"Why does this always end up happening between us?"

Sam knew it wasn't a rhetorical question. It was real. "Because you're gorgeous and sexy and we have amazing chemistry?"

Mindy rolled onto her side and swished her hand across his chest. "You're too enticing. I can't not kiss you. Which is a problem. I need to tell you something. Sophie and Emma were worried that I was going to fall under your spell."

Sam laughed. "I have a spell? I had no idea."

"Oh, you definitely do. You make me a little bit wild."

He reached out and cupped her bare shoulder, trailing his fingers down her arm. "Sweetheart, I'm pretty sure you're wild on your own. It's not my fault if I bring it out in you."

Mindy swatted his chest. "Let me finish. This is so stupid. I'm not even sure I can say it out loud."

"What?"

"My sisters and I made a bet that I won't fall for you again."

* * *

A Bet with Benefits is the third story
in The Eden Empire series.

Dear Reader,

Thanks for picking up *A Bet with Benefits*! It's the third Eden Empire book, about the heiresses of the Eden family, who are running their grandmother's Manhattan department store.

This story centers on Mindy, the eldest Eden sister. Mindy is as stuck as she can be—caught between her business, her sisters and the man who has an inexplicable hold on her, Sam Blackwell. Sam is Mindy's most pressing problem. She needs Sam to sell her a building for her business, and he needs an invitation to her sister's wedding to save face in NYC business circles. That's where the bet comes into play... Poor Mindy might be strong, but Sam is a formidable foe. In more ways than one!

The most fun of writing *A Bet with Benefits* came with Sam, who has spent two books being the villain. There's a lot more to this tall, handsome, mysterious man than we ever knew... Family secrets and family members(!) come to light, whether he likes it or not. Through that process, Mindy and Sam each learn to let down their guard and shed their facade. They are uniquely suited for each other and I loved writing their story.

I hope you enjoy this installment of the Eden Empire series. There's one more book after this one! Drop me a line anytime at karen@karenbooth.net. I love hearing from readers!

Karen

KAREN BOOTH

A BET WITH BENEFITS

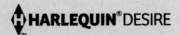

Recycling programs for this product may not exist in your area.

ISBN-13: 978-1-335-60389-0

A Bet with Benefits

Copyright © 2019 by Karen Booth

This edition published by arrangement with Harlequin Books S.A.

For questions and comments about the quality of this book, please contact us at CustomerService@Harlequin.com.

® and TM are trademarks of Harlequin Enterprises Limited or its corporate affiliates. Trademarks indicated with ® are registered in the United States Patent and Trademark Office, the Canadian Intellectual Property Office and in other countries.

Printed in U.S.A.

Karen Booth is a Midwestern girl transplanted in the South, raised on '80s music and repeated readings of *Forever* by Judy Blume. When she takes a break from the art of romance, she's listening to music with her nearly grown kids or sweet-talking her husband into making her a cocktail. Learn more about Karen at karenbooth.net.

Books by Karen Booth

Harlequin Desire

The Best Man's Baby
The Ten-Day Baby Takeover
Snowed in with a Billionaire

The Eden Empire

A Christmas Temptation
A Cinderella Seduction
A Bet with Benefits

Dynasties: Secrets of the A-List

Tempted by Scandal

Visit her Author Profile page at Harlequin.com, or karenbooth.net, for more titles.

You can find Karen Booth on Facebook, along with other Harlequin Desire authors, at Facebook.com/harlequindesireauthors!

For my sweet husband.
Every absurdly tall hero I write
is at least a little bit you.

One

Mindy Eden was doing far more than burning the candle at both ends—she was melting it from every angle. Her days were divided between her position as chief operating officer of her family's department store, Eden's, and her role as founder of her custom greeting card business, By Min-vitation Only, or BMO. Under Mindy's leadership, Eden's was rebounding after years of teetering on the edge, while BMO was growing by leaps and bounds. Money was rolling in, her to-do list was a mile long and she was sleeping about four hours a night. She loved every minute of it. This was no time to slow down for anything.

As she settled in the back seat of her car on her way to Eden's, her cell phone rang. She'd been waiting for this call from Matthew Hawkins, the interim chief executive officer Mindy had hired to run BMO while she helped her sisters get Eden's back on stable ground. "Matthew. Do you have news for me?"

"I do, and it's not what we were hoping for."

"Let me guess. They want more money." BMO had just made an offer on an amazing old warehouse in New Jersey. The Mercer Building. It was a massive space, and it would be a huge undertaking to move the entire company, but it had to be done. Right now, they had production running out of four different facilities, with the administrative offices at a fifth site and bulging at the seams. The Mercer would make it possible to streamline their entire operation and give them room to grow, and it would be an incredible space to work from.

"I wish it was as simple as that. The building has been sold," Matthew said flatly.

"What do you mean? I thought you were on top of this. You told me it was a done deal."

"Unfortunately, I think your personal life interfered on this one. Your *romantic* personal life."

Mindy was close to asking Matthew if he had his head screwed on right. There was no romance in her life. There wasn't much personal in there, either. Aside from the time she spent with her sisters, Sophie and Emma, at Eden's, she didn't have a spare minute to socialize. "Is this some sort of cruel joke?"

"Your ex. Sam Blackwell. He bought the building. Right out from under us."

Mindy was rarely caught off guard. She had a knack for anticipating problems and being a step ahead. But she had not seen this coming. Sam had been out of her life for five full months, since the last time she broke up with him and kicked him out of her apartment.

She'd never forget their last conversation.

You tell me to go and I'm not coming back. Ever.

My sisters need me more than I need you.

Have it your way, Min. Good luck with your dysfunctional family.

Mindy had broken up with Sam several times before that and he always found a way back. This time, he'd not only stayed away, he'd moved on to greener pastures. He'd been photographed with several gorgeous women in the tabloids, most recently with Valerie Cash, a former model turned executive fashion editor. That hadn't been easy for Mindy to take. She couldn't figure out what made him stay away this time. Unless, of course, it was because he'd finally believed her when she'd said that he was no good for her.

"Mindy? Are you there?" Matthew asked. "Sam Blackwell. Your ex-boyfriend."

"He was never my boyfriend." Sam never would've allowed himself such a label. He wasn't the type— his words, not hers.

"Look, I couldn't care less what role he played in your life. The bottom line is we have to start looking for something different. Maybe new construction. I can start meeting with architects and looking at commercial sites."

There was no way Mindy was going to give up on the Mercer this easily. "Are you insane? We're talking eighteen months on new construction, if we're lucky. We don't have that kind of time. And frankly, I'm a little shocked that you're suggesting it. That kind of delay could destroy everything I've built."

"With all due respect, I've built quite a lot since I've been here. I have a lot invested in BMO, as well."

Mindy had to stop herself from biting down on her own tongue. BMO was her company, not Matthew's. And he needed to stop acting this way. "I'm going to fix this. I don't want you to do another thing until you hear from me."

"How? The building is sold. If we try to buy it from Blackwell, he'll make us pay through the nose."

Mindy drew in a deep breath. Matthew was excellent at organization, but he wasn't much of a shark. She, however, was well versed in the art of getting what she wanted out of Sam Blackwell. Not that she was an expert. She'd failed at that before, but she at least knew his tricks. "Let me handle it. I'll let you know how it goes."

"This is technically my job."

And technically, I can fire you. "BMO is still my company and this affects our entire future. I want to get this done quickly, and I know how to deal with Sam."

"Good luck. I'd say you're going to need it."

Thanks for the big vote of confidence. "Good-bye, Matthew." Mindy leaned forward to speak to her driver, Clay. "Change of plans this morning. We need to make a stop before I head into Eden's. Eighteenth Street and Tenth Avenue. North side of the street."

"All the way down by Pier 60, Ms. Eden?"

"Yes, please. All the way down." *All the way down to see Sam.* Mindy sat back, glancing out the window and making a conscious effort to un-clench her jaw and relax her shoulders. She'd spent the last five months wondering if Sam Blackwell would find a way to wander back into her life. Now she had no choice but to storm into his. She would not allow him to create problems for her from afar, pulling strings and making messes. He was going to have to do it up close and personal.

"I won't be more than fifteen minutes," she

said when Clay pulled up in front of Sam's office building.

"Got it. I'll hang back and wait."

Mindy climbed out of the car, breathing in the crisp October day deeply, if only for a boost of confidence. She strode inside, sunglasses on and head held high. With no turnstile or guard in front of the elevator bank, she bypassed the security desk and nobody said a thing. Mindy had learned long ago that if you act as though you know where you're going, no one will question you. She did not want to give Sam even a minute to prepare for her arrival. She quickly scanned the directory and pressed the button for the seventh floor. Alone inside the elevator, she blew out a breath and decided to give herself a pep talk. "You got this. Sam Blackwell will not hurt you. Personally or professionally."

When the ding came and the door slid open, the reception desk was straight ahead, manned by a suitably gorgeous woman Mindy did not recognize. Behind her, a solid black wall was emblazoned with the words *S. Blackwell Enterprises* in gleaming chrome. The furnishings were sleek and modern, not so much as a stray paper clip in sight.

"May I help you?" the receptionist asked coldly.

"Mindy Eden for Sam."

"Is he expecting you?"

For an instant, Mindy considered answering honestly and saying no, but Sam had to be expecting her. He didn't do things like buy a building out from under someone unless he was expecting a response. "Yes. He is."

The receptionist picked up the phone and eyed Mindy as she spoke to Sam. "Yes, sir, Mr. Blackwell. Of course," she said before hanging up. "He'll be with you soon."

An eternity went by as Mindy paced in the reception area. Back and forth she went, but she wasn't about to sit down. She had too much anxiety coursing through her veins. The thought of seeing Sam made her nervous, a reaction she needed to stomp into submission. She would get what she wanted today. She would not let him control her.

She'd nearly convinced herself of it until all six feet and six inches of deliciously imposing Sam Blackwell appeared before her.

"Mindy." His voice was smooth and low, the sound filtering into her ears and quickly spreading through her entire body. It was like being gently shaken awake, something Sam had done to her countless times, rolling over in bed and pressing his long, lean form against hers. Sam was insatiable. He always wanted more of everything. Seeing him now made Mindy want to give him at least a little something. He was too appealing for words in black trousers and a charcoal-gray shirt, no tie, the sleeves rolled up to the elbows, showing off his firm forearms and his silver Rolex. His jet-black hair perfectly walked the line between tidy and messy. "I'd wondered when you'd turn up."

Damn him. So he *had* planned this. He'd lured her here by buying the Mercer and she'd taken the bait. Maybe she should have let Matthew deal with this, but it was too late for that. She had to stay strong. Confident. She couldn't let Sam rattle her. "I need fifteen minutes. In your office."

"That sounds like a lot more fun than what I was just working on." His eyebrows bounced, and the corners of his mouth threatened to curve into a smile.

Mindy cursed herself for thinking exactly what he was thinking. Fifteen minutes was plenty of time to do a lot of sexy things to each other. "If I do it right, it will only be fun for me."

"I've had worse offers." Sam waved Mindy closer, waiting until she started down the hall first. "Last door on the right."

"I remember." Mindy led the way, ignoring the intoxicating effect of having her lungs filled with Sam Blackwell–scented air, hoping she could find the strength to outmaneuver him and get the Mercer Building, all with her pride and heart intact.

Sam had a definite opinion about most things, but he was uncertain how to feel about Mindy Eden showing up at his office. Judging by the tug in the center of his chest the instant he saw her, he'd missed her. As he trailed behind her down the hall, the tension building in his hips confirmed that at the very least he'd missed her body—every killer curve. But he didn't trust Mindy. Not anymore. By the third time you get kicked out of a woman's life, she's officially taken the gloves off.

"What can I do for you?" Sam asked, closing the door behind him.

Mindy dropped her handbag in one of the chairs opposite his desk. "I had hoped you and I were beyond guessing games."

"If we are, it's because I don't play them. I honestly have no idea why you're here." He rounded his desk but waited to sit. "Please. Have a seat."

Mindy shook her head, her russet-red hair a wavy tumble across the shoulders of her trim-fitting black jacket. Peeking out from beneath her lapel was something black and lacy. He loved that she worked in a fashion-forward business and could apply a sexy edge to her wardrobe. "I'm not staying. I'm here about the Mercer Building. You know, the historic warehouse out in New Jersey that I was about to buy? You snatched it out from under me. You're trying to meddle in my business."

"I might have bought it, but it had nothing to do with your business."

Mindy's pouty berry-pink mouth went slack with disbelief. "So what, then? Was this some attempt to get back together with me?"

Wow. He had *not* seen that coming. "Is that really what you think?" He rounded his desk and closed in on her, enough to smell her perfume and see firsthand the touchable texture of her skin. His mind and body began to wage a battle. There was no telling which would win out—the urge to keep her at arm's length or the one to wrap her up in them. "I don't hear from you for five months and you think that I'm suddenly so struck with affection for you that I devise some silly plan to lure you to my office? Believe me, Mindy. If I wanted to get back together with you, I would call you. On the telephone. And I would ask you out."

Mindy crossed her arms as if she was determined to keep him away. "I have a hard time believing you aren't up to something, and it's not my fault that I suspect it. That's what you do. You meddle. You've interfered with Eden's plenty."

If only Mindy knew that what she saw as meddling, he considered to be nothing more than a favor. "I'm not a gatecrasher, Mindy, no matter what you think. I had nothing to do with buying that building out from under you. I don't know why Eden's would want it anyway. You have enough space in Manhattan to build a cruise ship."

"It's not for Eden's. It's for BMO. My company. We need to find a single space for our entire operation. Having things scattered all over the place is killing our margins."

That was a different case. BMO was Mindy's baby, but she'd left it in the hands of someone else. Had she managed to worm her way out of her duties at Eden's? Was that why she was taking time to personally address this issue? "I thought you were letting the interim CEO take the reins."

"I'm still involved in the day-to-day. I'm not really capable of being hands-off."

The phrase made Sam want to thread his fingers through Mindy's hair, but he pushed the thought aside. "I get that. I'm the same way."

"It's only a little more than a year until I will have fulfilled my two-year obligation to Eden's and can hightail it out of there. I'm not going to stop putting my mark on the world with BMO."

He'd always admired Mindy's determination. When she wanted something, she did *not* take her eyes off the prize. That had actually been part of the fun of being with her—trying to distract her. It almost always involved the two of them taking off each other's clothes. "Then how can I help? Do you want me to see if I can help you find a different space?"

"No. I want you to sell the Mercer Building to me."

He stepped back, perching on the very edge of his desk and stretching out his legs, crossing them at the ankles. He pinched his lower lip between his thumb and index finger. It wouldn't be a travesty if he decided to sell her the building, but Mindy was his key to an event he'd been certain before now he'd never get into. An event he needed to be at. "I need something in return." He didn't want to be greedy, but he also didn't want to be foolish. Why do a favor for Mindy? Out of the goodness of his heart? She'd ground his ego into the dirt with her stiletto heels. He didn't owe her a thing.

"A pile of money?"

"No. An invitation to your sister's wedding."

Mindy reared back her head, eyes wide with astonishment. "That's in a week. There are no invites to be had. Plus, why would you even want to go to Sophie's wedding? Half of the guest list doesn't like you."

Sam didn't hurt easily, but that wasn't an easy remark to hear. "It makes me look second-rate to not be attending the social event of the year."

"Since when do you care what people think about you?"

"A good businessperson always cares about their reputation. I've been concentrating my work in New York and I need to be firmly entrenched in those social circles if I'm going to get anything real done in this town." His sister, Isabel, had been the one to encourage him to stick closer to Manhattan over the last five months. She'd told him he couldn't outrun his feelings by buzzing to Prague or Buenos Aires or wherever the smell of money and big deals lured him. Logic said that the minute Mindy dumped him last time, he would want to be as far away as possible. The Eden family was impossible to ignore in this city. But he suspected Isabel was right. He couldn't avoid everything that caused him pain. Even when he'd had more than enough to last him a lifetime.

"I couldn't get an invitation for the queen of England right now. Sophie has been moaning for months about how tight the guest list is, and now that we're this close, she's perpetually freaking out."

Sam's mind immediately leaped to a solution. He cleared his throat and prepared himself for another potentially insulting answer. "Who's your date?"

A rush of pink colored Mindy's cheeks. She batted her lashes and looked away. "I don't have one. So what?"

"There's no need to be defensive about it." Sam had to fight the smile that wanted to cross his lips. He didn't want to be so happy that Mindy Eden, one of the most extraordinary women in the city, didn't have a date for her own sister's wedding. But he was. "I could fix that for you. You'd be killing two birds with one stone. Getting your building and a date."

"You'll really sell me the building if I take you to Sophie's wedding? That's all you want?"

Sam was surprised Mindy had asked the question, a classic misstep in negotiations. Never let on that you think you're getting a great deal. "Take me to the rehearsal dinner, too. You know, make it seem like I'm really in the inner circle."

"I'm not sure this is such a good idea. You and I both know we don't work as a couple."

Sam shrugged and pushed off from the desk, taking his seat behind it. He was wary of the idea, only because he knew how frustrating it would be to spend time with Mindy and not be able to touch her. But he could get some real business done at Sophie and Jake's wedding. He might even mend a few Eden fences. "Like I said, not struck with affection for you. But I think I could be convinced to keep you as a friend."

Mindy's blue-green eyes were full of questions, and maybe disappointment, too. He was okay with that. She'd taken him down many notches more than once. Let her know how much it hurt. "Okay. If you'll sell me the Mercer Building for what you paid, I will bring you to her wedding."

"And the rehearsal."

"I'll have to figure out how to play it with Sophie, but okay. The rehearsal, too."

"For what I paid?"

"Yes. Not a penny more."

"And as friends."

She grumbled and plucked her handbag from the chair, hooking it on her arm. "If that's what we're shooting for, then yes. Friends."

Sam got up to walk her out.

"I can find my way," she shot at him.

"I know that. I just want to be sure you don't steal anything on your way out."

"Very funny."

"Okay, then. You go ahead. I'll just watch." He leaned against the door frame, grinning to himself. Their impromptu meeting had been a win for him, especially the last part. He'd come off like a gentleman, when really he'd been after only a spectacular eyeful as Mindy walked away.

Two

As Mindy left Sam's office, only one thought was running through her head: *What in the hell did I just agree to?* Letting Sam be her date to Sophie's wedding? On a long list of bad ideas, this not only belonged at the very top, it was the entire reason for making a list in the first place. Sam was trouble. Her family, for all intents and purposes, hated him. He was the king of underhanded behavior, which he always managed to explain away as somehow noble or good. Then there was the unavoidable fact that Mindy seemed to lose about fifty points off her IQ when she was around him. He had a real talent for making her do stupid things. Case in point, agreeing to let him take her to Sophie's wedding.

Judging by the way she'd felt during their short meeting, it wouldn't be hard for him to do it to her again. Her physical attraction to him was still off the charts. That was why she hadn't taken a seat, even when her brand-new Louboutins were killing her feet. She couldn't allow herself to linger or get comfortable, even when she'd wanted nothing more than to unbutton her jacket and ask him if he wanted to rekindle the flame between them. One more time. For old times' sake. But Sam was too sly and clever. Whip-smart and devious. There were plenty of reasons to stay away.

Of course, he'd been clear that attending the wedding together would be only as friends. That one detail of their agreement had helped her decide she could escape this scenario unscathed. So she'd be on the arm of a ridiculously hot guy for a few nights, she wouldn't have to go stag to Sophie's wedding and she'd get the building her business so desperately needed. This was a win-win-win. As long as she kept her clothes on and her head out of the clouds.

Clay whisked Mindy off to Eden's, dropping her off at the south entrance on Thirty-Sixth Street. She breezed through the store, past cosmetics and the perfume girls, through ladies' accessories to the back elevators that would take her up to the executive offices. She still hadn't figured out how to handle this news with Sophie, although she had an idea

about an approach involving one of Jake's grooms-
men, Gerald, and his wandering hands.

"Hey, Soph," Mindy said, knocking on Sophie's
doorway, which was almost always open. "Do you
have a minute?"

"Sure. I can't keep my mind on work right now
anyway." Her sister pushed back from her desk,
gathering her sleek red locks in her hand and pulling them in a bundle over one shoulder. Always
fashionable and put-together, Sophie was wearing
a jade green floral dress with dramatic bell sleeves.

Mindy was making herself at home on Sophie's
gray velvet sofa when Emma appeared at the door.

"Discussing wedding stuff, by any chance?" she
asked.

"Yes. Actually. That's exactly why I wanted to
talk to Sophie." Mindy patted the seat next to her.
"Join us."

"You guys want to talk about the wedding?" Sophie asked, incredulous. "I always feel like I'm jam-
ming it down your throat."

Emma glanced over at Mindy and without words,
conveyed their shared desire for the relief they
would feel when Sophie's wedding was over. "Oh,
no. We love to talk about the wedding," Emma said,
putting on an excellent front.

"It's the best part of the day," Mindy lied.

Emma tucked her long chocolate-brown hair behind her ear and crossed her legs, showing off an in-

credible pair of cherry-red Manolo Blahnik pumps. The three sisters did enjoy outdoing each other when it came to shoes, although this was a daring choice for the otherwise more subdued Emma. Her charcoal tweed pencil skirt and jacket made a nice counterpoint. "Absolutely. Mindy, what's your news?"

Mindy wasn't about to stall. She wanted to get this over with. "I found a date for the wedding. If you can just let Jake know and have him somehow filter that news down to Gerald, that would be great."

"Why don't you tell Gerald yourself? Doesn't he text you four or five times a day?"

This was true. Gerald had been putting the full-court press on Mindy from the moment he met her at the first engagement party. He was one of Jake's business school pals, and Sophie had known him then, as well. He had it in his head that Jake and Sophie along with Mindy and Gerald would make the perfect pair of power couples. Mindy had been clear that she wasn't interested, but she'd delivered that news gently, only because she knew she was going to see Gerald a lot at the various events leading up to the wedding. Apparently she'd been too soft with her approach. Gerald didn't seem to be taking the hint.

"Yes. He does. I just don't know how to work that particular detail into a text conversation."

"Then call him," Sophie said.

"I don't want to encourage him. And this was all your idea in the first place. Telling me to get a date to send him a signal."

"So?" Emma knocked Mindy's knee with her own. "Who's the guy?"

Mindy couldn't afford to hesitate with her answer. "Sam."

The room went dead silent. Mindy braced for the fallout.

"No. No way," Sophie said. "Absolutely not."

"What? You can't tell me who I can bring as a date. I'm a grown woman."

"Not around Sam you aren't. And it's my wedding. I don't like Sam. My future husband despises him. And frankly, you shouldn't like him, either. Just think about the things he's done to interfere with our business." Sophie gestured to Emma. "Or our own sister, for that matter. He was the one who leaked the story of Emma's childhood to the tabloids."

"Which was ultimately a good thing, wasn't it?" Mindy turned to Emma, pleading with her eyes.

"It was." Emma looked back and forth between Mindy and Sophie, seeming stuck. "I just wish I would've had the chance to do it myself."

"See? There you go." Sophie sat back in her chair. "You are not bringing Sam Blackwell to my wedding. If nothing else, he is going to stomp all over your heart, and I am not going to watch that happen again."

"Ah, but see, that won't be a problem. We agreed that we're only attending as friends."

"Why in the world would you even want to be friends with him? Does he have any friends? Is he capable of it?" Sophie asked.

Mindy had been afraid of that question, but she'd anticipated it. She considered telling Emma and Sophie about the deal for the Mercer Building, but that seemed like news for after the wedding. She didn't want to give them any more reasons to question his motives. "Whatever you think of him, we were good friends. We understand each other, at least from a business standpoint. And I couldn't find a date. That's the very sad reality of my life right now. I know you think Gerald is harmless, but I'd like to keep him at bay."

Sophie nodded, seeming to think hard about all of this. Emma sat back and wrapped her arms around her middle.

"What, you guys? Just tell me what you're thinking. I can take it."

"Even if it all goes fine, even if there are no problems, I worry about you and Sam together, especially in a romantic environment like a wedding," Sophie said softly.

"It's true. It's hard not to get caught up in the romanticism. And you were so sad after the last time you and Sam broke up," Emma added.

"I broke up with him because I couldn't be in any way disloyal to you guys. I told him as much. And of course I was sad, but we've had five months apart and I think we're ready to be friends." Mindy doubted whether that was at all possible, but she had to try, at least to get the Mercer Building.

"I'm worried you'll fall for him again. Then you'll be miserable. Again," Sophie said.

"I won't."

"You will."

"I will not," Mindy insisted.

"Wanna bet?" Sophie asked.

"I told you I won't fall for him," Mindy restated.

"Then bet me. I know you and you hate to lose. So we'll make a bet and as long as you don't lose it, you won't get hurt." Sophie grabbed the pencil on her desk and began tapping it against a legal pad. "The question is what to bet."

"I know," Emma said. "The one thing Mindy doesn't want, to stay at Eden's longer than she has to."

Mindy was struck with horror while Sophie's expression became one of sheer delight. "Yes. That's perfect." Sophie clapped her hands together gleefully. "You promise me there will be no romance between you and Sam, and I will stop pestering you about staying on at Eden's beyond the deadline next year."

"And if I lose?" Mindy asked, wary of the whole thing.

"Then you have to stay for one more year. That should give Emma and me enough time to convince you to stay full-time."

Mindy was starting to feel trapped, a feeling she didn't handle well. Sophie and Emma had both been making their case for Mindy to sell BMO and stay at Eden's. But maybe this bet could be a good one. It would keep her from falling under Sam's spell. The very last thing she wanted was to spend an extra year at Eden's. The second-to-last thing she wanted was to deal with Sophie's and Emma's regular hints about her staying.

"We're talking a real bet, you two." Mindy pointed back and forth between Sophie and Emma. "You guys don't get to say one more thing to me about walking away from BMO if I'm able to keep Sam in the friend zone. Not a peep. No guilt trips. Nothing."

Emma nodded. "I'm good with it."

"Me, too," Sophie said.

"Fine. It's settled." Mindy got up from her seat, feeling pretty good about having gotten everything she needed out of a second meeting today. "Oh, and just so you know, I'm planning on bringing Sam to the rehearsal dinner."

"Seriously?" Sophie asked.

"Yes. Just think of it as one more chance for you

to win your bet." Mindy stopped at the door and turned to Emma. "I almost forgot. Emma, did you have something you wanted to talk about?"

Emma noticeably winced. "I guess my mom and your mom had a phone conversation. It didn't go well. Your mom hung up on mine." Jenny Stewart, Emma's mom, and Jill Eden, Sophie and Mindy's mom, had a complicated relationship. They were sisters. Who didn't speak to each other. They'd also each had children by the same man, making Emma not only Sophie and Mindy's cousin, but their half sister, as well. It was a bizarre situation, to say the least. All three sisters had hoped that the occasion of Sophie's wedding and the fact that they were all working together now might be a reason for the moms to make amends. Apparently not.

"Is this going to be a problem at the wedding?" Sophie asked. "I don't think I can handle any more stress."

Emma shook her head. "I figure I'll handle my mom and Mindy can handle yours. As long as we keep them apart, it should be fine. There might be some steely silence, but that should be the extent of the drama. I promise we'll keep everything going smoothly."

Sophie took a deep breath, her shoulders rising and falling. "Okay, then. Let's hope this all goes off without a hitch."

* * *

Sam couldn't keep Mindy off his mind, even though he had a mountain of work to do. *This will be a good thing*, he kept saying to himself, although he wasn't 100 percent sure. Attending Sophie and Jake's wedding certainly had the potential to put Sam back into a few business and social circles he'd managed to spin himself out of. But he also worried there was something else to it. Every time he read about the upcoming nuptials, it sent him into a downward spiral, thinking about Mindy's life and wondering what she was doing and—most important—whom she was dating. He'd jumped at the chance to stake his claim on Mindy the instant he realized she didn't have a date. But there was no claiming Mindy. She was her own person, through and through. Would this wedding just end up being an exercise in public humiliation? Quite possibly. But without risk came no reward. And he knew that his bad relationship with the Eden family had to end. It was keeping him from making all of the money he wanted to make.

Sam jumped when his phone line buzzed.

"Mr. Blackwell. Mindy Eden is on the line for you." It was almost as if she knew he'd been thinking about her.

"Mindy, hi. Two conversations in one day. I hardly know what to make of this."

"I won't keep you long if that's what you're worried about."

"Believe me, I'm not worried."

"I was calling to give you the details of the rehearsal dinner and the wedding. I tried to reach you on your cell, but some woman answered and told me to call you at the office. Please tell me that wasn't Valerie Cash I just spoke to. I refuse to go with a taken man to my sister's wedding."

Sam pursed his lips to stifle a laugh. Mindy did have a bit of a jealous streak. "Valerie and I are no longer dating. It was a very short-lived thing."

"Long enough to be in the tabloids more than once."

So she *was* jealous. If that was the case, why hadn't she tried to beat Valerie Cash at her own game? He would've given in without too much of a fight. Okay…a little fight. But now? Months later? He wasn't feeling generous. "It's over. That's all you need to know." He swallowed hard and prepared himself for the question he had to ask. "How'd you manage to keep your love life under wraps that whole time?"

Mindy laughed quietly. "Cute, Sam. Real cute."

"What?"

"Nice attempt at digging for information. I'm not about to tell you what I've been up to. I'd rather keep the mystery alive. Also, I'd rather ask about the mysterious woman answering your phone."

"It's one of my assistants. My phone has been acting up, so she's out getting me a new one."

Several seconds of silence wound its way through the line. "Oh. Okay."

Sam couldn't help but notice how uncertain Mindy sounded. Had she really been bothered that much by his relationship with Valerie? Had that been what kept her away? "So the wedding. Do you want to just text me the details?"

"Sure. I can do that. You should know that since the wedding is taking place at the Grand Legacy Hotel, I'm staying there both nights. If you wanted to do that, you could book a room. It would just need to be a separate room. And I don't know what their availability is."

"Right. Friends and all."

"Exactly."

"I think I'll sleep in my own bed those nights." *It will save me the temptation.* "So how did Sophie take the news that I was coming?"

"She wasn't superexcited, but she was fine. Don't worry about my sister. She'll be too drunk on love and attention to know what's going on. You just play the part of model wedding guest and we'll be fine."

"I do know how to behave in social situations, you know."

"I know. I guess I'm just restating the obvious." Mindy blew out a breath of frustration. "I should go. My to-do list is ridiculous."

"Oh, sure. Me, too." For some reason, Sam couldn't bring himself to say goodbye and he sensed that Mindy was feeling the same way. "Big plans this weekend?"

"Sleeping, perhaps. Maybe brunch on Sunday. How about you?"

"Definitely the sleeping part. You know how I feel about brunch."

"You're the only person I know who doesn't like it." Despite her words, Mindy's voice was light and playful.

"Well, which is it? Breakfast? Or lunch? Make up your mind, brunch. You don't get to be both. Plus, it's basically cutting out an entire meal, which is a big downside for me. I will always eat."

"I actually noticed today that you were looking a bit skinny. Are you sure you've been eating?"

Sam ran his hand over his stomach. He hadn't weighed himself in forever, but he had noticed that his pants were getting a bit loose. "Clearly not enough if you think I'm looking scrawny."

"I didn't say *scrawny*. I said *skinny*. You're still all muscle."

Sam had to swallow back a groan. The thought of Mindy looking at him that closely was a definite turn-on. One he knew he shouldn't be relishing too much. "I'm not sure friends should be making comments about each other's bodies."

"It was just an observation," Mindy retorted.

"Fair enough. For the record, you looked perfect today." *Every last inch.*

"You're just sucking up to me because I'm taking you to the wedding of the year."

Not really. "You've always seen right through me, Mindy Eden. I can't get a single thing past you, can I?"

Mindy laughed again, a musical sound that made Sam feel a little lighter. "Nope. So you'd better stay on your toes. I'll call you next week so we can make a plan for the rehearsal on Friday."

"Sounds perfect."

Sam and Mindy said their goodbyes, but as soon as he hung up, his office line buzzed again. "Mr. Blackwell? There's a Ms. Parson on the phone. She won't tell me who she's with or what she's calling about, but she's very insistent that she needs to speak with you."

Sam was more than a little annoyed by this. Just when he'd been having fun talking to Mindy, he had to be smacked in the face with a less-than-pleasant call. "Put her through."

"Mr. Blackwell?" Ms. Parson asked.

"I thought I asked you to never call me at the office."

"You did, and I'm sorry, but I was unable to reach you on your cell phone."

"Yeah. Sorry about that. Long story."

"Well, I'm very sorry to bother you during the

day. I was as discreet as I could be when I called."
Ms. Parson had always kept Sam's business with
her a secret, at his request.

"It's fine. What can I do for you?"

"I know your involvement with our organization
has always been anonymous, but there's a potential
problem with the couple who is underwriting and
hosting this year's big event. Do you know who and
what I'm talking about?"

Sam had heard inklings of this. "The senator
and her husband. Something about a sex scandal?"

"Yes. I'm afraid so. Obviously, if that continues
to play out the way it is in the tabloids, we're going
to have to ask them to step aside. Which means we
will need a new host for the event. You'd be the
perfect person to do it. You've been such a big con-
tributor for so long."

Sam drew in a deep breath. He'd attended this
event many times and was well aware of what hosting it involved—getting up in front of a crowd of
five hundred people and asking them to open their
wallets, usually by telling a story that caused people
to reach for a tissue. "That would require me to step
into the spotlight. I prefer to keep my personal life,
especially my past, out of the public eye."

"I know that, Mr. Blackwell. And we've always
respected your wishes. Always. But perhaps it's
time to be a bit more public about your involvement.
People might benefit from hearing your story, es-

pecially since your mother was so young when she passed away."

"I'll think about it. No promises." Sam hung up, swallowed hard and looked out the window. He didn't like to think about this. It was too painful. He preferred to write a sizable check every year, try very hard to forget the difficult parts of his past and to remember happier times. Those days were so far gone, it was sometimes hard to believe they'd ever existed. His sister, Isabel, was the only person on the planet still around to remind him that any of it had ever been real.

Three

Sam's driver dropped him off in front of the Grand Legacy Hotel on Forty-Fifth Street, a few blocks west of the bright lights and perpetual hustle of Times Square. The night air held just a hint of cooler fall weather, but Sam would take what he could get. Summer in New York was insufferable. He was glad to see it gone.

Sam had always admired the Grand Legacy, an art deco jewel brought back to life by fellow real estate developer Sawyer Locke and his brother, Noah. Sam was hoping to get some face time with them both tomorrow during the wedding reception, along with many other notable members of that business circle. Spending more time in New York over the last several months had meant confronting a lot of his earliest misdeeds in business. He could admit that he'd been a little too ruthless more than once. He wished that hadn't been the case, but when you'd been on your own since the age of seventeen, you became a survivalist. You took as much as you could, even if it meant amassing more money than you could ever spend. Every dollar in the bank was another layer of security. Now that he was thirty-six, he was starting to see the errors of his ways. He wanted to mend a few fences, especially with Jake Wheeler, Sophie's fiancé.

Sam stepped into the lobby and straightened his jacket as he scanned the crowd ahead, a throng of people talking and mingling near the hotel's grand staircase, which led up to the main bar, the hotel's speakeasy during prohibition. He'd dressed in a charcoal-gray suit, white shirt and midnight-blue tie—quite a conservative getup for a guy who preferred to wear only the darkest colors, black if he could get away with it. For the first time in his life, he was making an effort to blend in rather than lurk in the shadows.

It took him only a few seconds to spot Mindy. Being a head taller than most people afforded him the luxury, and he took full advantage of the view. She was simply stunning in a black cocktail dress, her scarlet-red hair framing her flawless face in shiny waves. As he moved through the crowd to reach her, he saw that she was having a conversation with a man he didn't recognize. He knew that look on her face—her lips pulled tight in a thin smile. She wasn't happy. The man put his arm around her and kissed her cheek. Mindy recoiled and Sam was ready to push past several people to save her, but she turned her head and spotted him, her eyes flashing bright. She muttered something to the man, then quickly wound her way to Sam.

"You're here!" she exclaimed, throwing her arms around his neck and pulling him forward until he had no choice but to kiss her square on the lips. "We're going to have to abandon that whole just-friends thing," she muttered against his mouth.

Sam reflexively wrapped his arms around her waist, his lips buzzing from the kiss. Mindy flattened herself against his chest, making everything in his body go tight. "What happened?" he asked, mumbling into her ear. Her silky hair brushed his cheek. Her skin was so soft and warm. He knew then that no matter what she said to him next, this wedding was going to be a test.

Mindy released him from her embrace but quickly tucked herself under his arm, placing her hand on his stomach. "See that guy I was talking to?" she asked out of the side of her mouth.

Sam cast his sights down at her, loving the view the deep V of her neckline gave him. "I couldn't help but notice. He seems to like you." Sure enough, Sam casually glanced at the man, who was narrowly watching them while he stabbed ice cubes in a glass with a cocktail stirrer.

"That's Gerald Van Dyke. One of the grooms-men. For some unknown reason, he has a big thing for me. I keep telling him I'm not interested, but he thinks I'm kidding. Like he can't seem to fathom it."

"He's a good-looking guy. He's probably not used to women turning him down."

Mindy gazed up at him. "And he's loaded, too. So I'm sure he thinks I'm nuts for not being inter-ested, but he's just not my type."

"I wasn't aware that you had a type."

Mindy shook her head at him. "Take a look in the mirror and you'll know exactly what I have a big weakness for."

Sam appreciated knowing that he was at least physically what Mindy wanted, but that almost cast their past in a worse light. Had it been nothing more than sex to her? Her propensity for ordering him out of her apartment made him think yes. "Do you typi-cally kick guys who are your type out of your life?"

"I had no choice when you were messing with my family. Especially since none of them are par-ticularly fond of you because of it. And I still don't buy your excuse that you were trying to make me happy."

Sam knew then how little Mindy understood

him. "Why? Do you truly believe that I don't care about the happiness of others?"

"It's not that so much as you don't seem like the kind of guy who would try to save someone. Especially more than once."

"There are lots of things you don't know about me, Mindy." He'd have to leave it at that.

"Yeah? Because I feel like you're an open book." She again made eye contact, her expression nothing but clear conviction. "It's one of the things I like most about you. You always tell me exactly what you're thinking."

Not even close. Out of the corner of his eye, Sam could see that Sophie and Jake were making their way closer to them. "This might be a conversation for another time."

"Right. Well, regardless, you and I need to pretend like we like each other a lot. Just until Gerald gets on a plane back to Miami."

Sam leaned down and kissed Mindy's temple, hoping Gerald would take the hint. "I think I remember how to do that." *I have a lot of practice.*

"Good." Mindy faced him again and smoothed her hand across his chest, sending a tidal wave of warmth through his body. This no-longer-friends plan of hers might kill him. "I hope you can keep it up for a few days."

Sam settled his hand in the small of her back and pulled her against him. Their physical proximity was doing more than make him miss what they'd had before. He felt almost desperate to reclaim it. If only for one night. "You know I can keep it up long enough to make you very happy."

One corner of her luscious mouth pulled into a smile. "Clever. I also forgot to mention that you might have to stay here with me tonight and tomorrow."

Now Sam knew he was truly in trouble. He and Mindy wouldn't last two seconds behind closed doors. It was a miracle they hadn't torn off each other's clothes a week ago in his office. "I feel like you're breaking every parameter of our agreement."

"I'm sorry, but Gerald's room is across the hall from mine. I'm not sure a do-not-disturb sign will be enough to keep him from knocking on my door or slipping creepy notes under it."

"So you need me to be your muscle."

"I prefer to think of you as a stunt boyfriend."

Sam laughed at the joke, but these were dangerous waters to be wading into with Mindy. Why did he have to be so drawn to the one woman who was most likely to take everything she wanted from him with absolutely no guarantees of anything else?

Mindy was digging herself a deeper hole with every passing minute in Sam's very capable arms, but she had no choice. She'd never be able to enjoy her sister's wedding if Gerald was pestering her.

However much she and Emma had complained about Sophie while she'd been planning the wedding, they both very much wanted it to be a perfect affair. This was a time for celebration.

"Sophie and Jake are coming this way," Sam mumbled into her ear.

Unfortunately, staying away from Gerald by staying close to Sam was only going to convince Sophie that Mindy had fallen under his spell again. For the moment, Mindy was stuck between the rock that was Sam and the hard place that was her sister.

"Jake. Sophie. Congratulations." Sam gave Sophie a quick hug, then shook Jake's hand. The two men were quickly locked in a steely-eyed staring contest.

"Thank you, Sam," Sophie said, bugging her eyes at Mindy. "Don't you two look cozy over in this quiet corner." It wasn't a question. It was a statement.

"The lobby is packed. Everybody's cozy," Mindy countered, knowing she'd have to explain to Sophie that she and Sam were canoodling in public only out of necessity.

Jake stood back and put his arm around Sophie. Sam stuffed his hands into his pockets. Mindy felt an urgent need to remedy the distinct lack of conversation. "The rehearsal went well. I'm sure tomorrow will be amazing."

Sophie smiled, but Mindy could see the unease

on her face. Was it prewedding jitters or did she truly despise Sam that much? "I hope everything goes off as planned. I don't want to have to stress at all."

"Everything will be perfect," Mindy replied. "If there are any problems, Emma and I will deal with them."

"So, Jake, how's business these days?" Sam asked. For a moment it felt as if they were all holding their breath, waiting for the answer.

Jake allowed the corners of his mouth to turn up, but it wasn't even close to being a real smile. "Better than ever, although I'm surprised you'd ask. It's one thing for you to show up at my wedding as Mindy's date, and quite another for you to ask about business. As if you actually care about that part of my life."

Mindy was shocked by Jake's tone. She knew he didn't like Sam, but this was more biting than she'd ever heard from him. She looked to Sophie for answers, but her sister was pursing her lips and avoiding eye contact.

"Come on, Jake," Sam replied. "That was a long time ago. You shouldn't hold on to animosities for so long. You're getting married to an amazing woman. This should be a happy time."

Before Mindy had a chance to figure out what was transpiring between Sam and her future brother-in-law, Jake had dropped his hold on Sophie and was nearly toe-to-toe with Sam. "You don't get to tell me what to do. Especially not about my work or my personal life."

"Jake. Stop. What is going on with you?" Sophie tugged on Jake's arm.

He cast an uncharacteristically mean-spirited look at Mindy. "Your sister brought a jerk to our wedding. That's what's wrong."

"Hey. Jake. That's not cool," Mindy said. "And don't talk like that. You'll just upset Sophie."

Sam reached for Mindy's hand. "No. No. It's okay." He then turned to Sophie while Mindy thought her heart was going to punch a hole in her chest. Her pulse was racing. "Sophie, apparently Jake never told you that he and I were almost business partners at one point. A long time ago."

"We were more than possible business partners, Sam. We were friends. And we never became partners because Sam talked me out of going in with him on what ended up being his first big deal. He made a mint and completely cut me out of the profits."

Was this the root of the dissension between Jake and Sam? It certainly sounded like something Sam would do. A person didn't get a ruthless reputation by being anything less than cutthroat.

From across the room came the sound of clinking glass. "Ladies and gentlemen, if you can all begin moving into the restaurant's private dining room, we'll be serving dinner soon."

"Look. We have to go." Sophie seemed nothing less than flustered, which Mindy hated seeing. "I guess we'll see you two later. Just, please, no drama."

Jake and Sophie blazed a trail through the crowd while Sam pulled Mindy aside.

"Maybe this wasn't such a good idea. I think I underestimated how much Jake is still holding a grudge."

"Did you really screw him over?"

Sam took in a deep breath through his nose. "I wouldn't characterize it quite like that. We were both getting our businesses off the ground. Neither of us really knew what we were doing."

Was this Sam covering his tracks? He had a way of seeing his own misdeeds in quite a different light than others. "Cutting a friend out of a deal is no small thing. And you're a smart guy. I don't buy for a minute that you didn't know that because you were only starting out."

He nodded in agreement, but the tension on his face was clear. "You're right. You're absolutely right. I had my reasons for doing it, though."

"Can you tell me what they were?"

"This was years ago, Mindy. I don't really want to dredge up the past."

"And I get that, but Jake is clearly still angry

about it, and he's marrying my sister, so I feel like I deserve to know your side. So I can at least defend you. That is, if you deserve defending." She still didn't trust Sam completely, but she did feel like she'd learned more about him during their last two conversations than she'd ever known about him. She couldn't help but want to push for more. It was just her way.

"Tell you what. I'll explain it later."

"Later tonight? When you come to my room?"

"Yeah. About that. I'm not so sure that's a good idea. How about I walk you up to your room and sneak out when it looks like the coast is clear?"

Mindy hated the disappointment that came with Sam's answer, but it was the sensible choice and she was determined to be nothing but smart about Sam. "I'll take what I can get from you, Sam Blackwell."

"I expect nothing less."

Sam and Mindy made their way into the dining room and took their seats, across the table from Jake and Sophie. All Mindy could do was hope that Sophie wasn't feeling as on edge as she was, but judging by the number of glasses of champagne Sophie had downed, she was working hard to smooth her ragged edges. As difficult as it was for Mindy to imagine herself as the bride-to-be, she tried to put herself in her sister's shoes. If she was getting married, she definitely wouldn't want to endure any hostility between her groom and her sister's date.

This was Sophie's time, and Mindy needed to stay focused on doing everything she could to help make it perfect.

As dessert was served, the toasts were announced by Jake's best man, who gently clinked a spoon against his wineglass. Mindy listened to his sweet and sentimental words for the happy couple, hoping she could measure up. She didn't want to let her sister down. When it came time for Mindy's turn, Sophie reached across the table and squeezed her hand.

"I hope you know how much I love you," Sophie said quietly.

Tears immediately welled in Mindy's eyes. She nodded eagerly. "Me, too. I love you so much." She stood and raised her glass, trying to run through her carefully crafted toast, while the realization of her predicament settled over her. Even if she took Sam and the bet with her sisters out of it, the reality was that she and Sophie and Emma were bound tight, and that bond was getting stronger every day. It was going to be ridiculously hard to walk away from Eden's in a year. Even when that had always been Mindy's plan. Even when that was what she'd wanted all along, there would be no easy way out.

"I want to say that I'm incredibly lucky to have the best sisters in the world. We don't always agree or get along, but at the end of the day, I know that they both have my back." She turned to Sophie, trying to ward off the lump that was forming in her throat. They had been through so much together, and it was time to recognize that. "Sophie, you and I have been thick as thieves since the minute Mom and Dad brought you home from the hospital. You have always been fiercely loyal and full of the best intentions. Nobody deserves to have found true love more than you. I know that you and Jake will have a long and loving life together, and I couldn't be happier for you."

Everyone in the dining room offered a hearty "Hear, hear!" Mindy knocked back the last of her champagne, then became fixed on the sight of Jake and Sophie. They exchanged a sweet kiss, then looked deeply into each other's eyes. It was so easy to see that there was nothing but love and admiration between them. Mindy didn't want to be envious, but there was an invisible force pulling at her and leaving her feeling empty inside. She turned to Sam, only to see that he was watching them, too. He glanced over at Mindy, shrugged, then slugged back the last of his drink. Did he think this was all unbelievably sappy? Too sweet? If so, what had made Sam so hardened to the world? Was it simply years of pursuing big deals with no regard for the toll? Had his immense success made him not care about the more important things in life?

As the guests began to dwindle, Sam got up from his seat. "I'm pretty tired, so if you're still wanting me to walk you up to your room, it would be great if we could go now."

Mindy saw that Sophie and Jake were deep in conversation. Emma and her fiancé, Daniel, had already left. "Okay. Sure."

They strolled back through the lobby to the bank of elevators. With no one around, there was no show to put on, which meant no hand-holding. Mindy reminded herself this was for the best. She'd navigate whatever rockiness there was tomorrow, buy the building from Sam and then decide if she and he could make a run at friendship. That seemed like something Sam really needed, especially after witnessing his run-in with Jake, even if he might not ever admit it. Still, friendship meant closeness, and that would require a delicate balance. It was a narrow path to walk with Sam. It was so easy to get lured back in.

Mindy keyed into her ninth-floor suite, Sam following behind her. Before he let the door shut, he took the do-not-disturb sign and hung it on the outside knob.

"Can I make you a drink?" she asked, again filled with this uncomfortable mix of hope and regret. She hoped he'd stay, but she regretted her inclination to think that way. Why did her brain have to go there?

He leaned against the wall and again stuffed

his hands into his pockets. "I'm okay. I won't stay long."

"What if you run into Gerald in the hall?"

Sam flashed her a devilish smile. "I'll tell him I'm running out for condoms."

Mindy laughed, but she had to force it out of herself. Her ill-advised hopes had officially been dashed. "Well, thank you for tonight. I know it wasn't easy. Are you sure you don't want to tell me about the Jake situation?"

He shook his head slightly and stared down at the floor. "Not right now. It's not a big deal. He'll get over it or he won't. I have no control over what other people think of me."

Mindy wasn't used to this more somber side of Sam. "Okay. Well, if you ever want to talk about it, I'm all ears. Superunderstanding and completely nonjudgmental ears."

He smiled, a breathy laugh crossing his lips. "I appreciate that."

"Any time."

"Gotta be nice to the guy whose building you so desperately want to buy. Right?"

Mindy dropped her head to one side and stepped closer to him. "It's more than that. I hope you know that."

He nodded, but judging by the look in his eyes, he wasn't necessarily buying it. "I should head out."

"Okay. Sure. Thanks for coming tonight."

"Absolutely. I'll see you tomorrow." He leaned down and pressed a soft kiss to her temple, gently gripping her shoulders. That brush of his skin sent tiny shock waves through her—pulses of electricity meant to remind her that he knew how to make her unravel. He could be her undoing.

And just like that, Sam slipped through the door to her hotel room, the door thudding shut. Mindy wandered over to the bed, kicked off her shoes and flopped back on the mattress, staring up at the ceiling. Tonight had not gone the way she'd thought it would. Some parts were better. Some parts were decidedly worse. More than anything, she was starting to see Sam in a different light. She'd always thought of him as an open book. Now she was starting to think that she might have read only the first chapter.

Four

Sam had thought once or twice about skipping Jake and Sophie's wedding. It had taken far too much self-control to walk out of Mindy's room last night. If things had been different, he would have stayed. But he wasn't ready to be pulled back into Mindy's world, however much it made him look good to be at this wedding. He wanted her, but he didn't. Part of him wanted a fuller life, and part of him wasn't convinced it was worth the hassle. In his experience, people you dare to care about eventually leave, in one way or another. In Mindy's case, they banish you from their life and pull you back in only when it suits them.

He arrived at the Grand Legacy early. Which was

a good thing, judging by the panic-stricken look on Mindy's face as she rushed across the lobby to him. "I'm so glad you're here a little early. Gerald is being ridiculous. He won't leave me alone." She glanced back over her shoulder, seemingly making sure the coast was clear.

The situation *was* ridiculous. Sam had to put it to an end. "Where is he? Let me talk to him and tell him to back off."

"You can't make a scene, Sam. Sophie is already freaking out enough as it is. Plus, I don't think Jake will like it if you're mean to one of his best friends."

Sam grumbled under his breath and pushed aside his annoyance, instead taking his chance to admire her—she was breathtaking in a flowing dove-gray bridesmaid's dress that showed off her glowing sculpted shoulders and graceful collarbone. "I can't entirely blame Gerald. You look especially beautiful today, Min."

Mindy dropped her stressed facade for an instant, while her rosy pink lips pulled into a pleased smile. "Thank you. You clean up very well. I love you in a tux. I don't think I've ever seen you wear one before." She smoothed her hand over his lapel and dragged her fingers down the length of his arm.

"I'm not a huge fan, but I figured your stunt boyfriend would wear one."

"You're absolutely right. He would. Now come on. Stay close to me." Mindy grabbed his hand and began pulling him back across the lobby toward the bank of elevators. "Gerald's not our only problem today, unfortunately. I think we have a potential catfight on our hands."

"Our problem? Don't you mean your problem? I'd been hoping to do some networking today. Reconnect with a few big fish."

"But I need your help."

Sam didn't completely understand why he allowed himself to be pulled into Eden family drama. He only knew that it happened with regularity. "Alright. I suppose you'd better tell me why there's going to be a catfight." If today was going to be torture, and wholly unproductive from a business standpoint, at least it would be interesting.

"There's trouble brewing between my mom and Emma's mom," Mindy muttered, stopping and pulling him closer. "They're already throwing around unkind words and I'm worried about what's going to happen when champagne starts flowing at the reception. This is only the second time they've been in the same room since our grandmother died and her will was read."

"You mean the day everyone found out they'd both had children by your dad?"

"Exactly."

Other than his sister, Sam had no extended family to speak of. His father had passed away when he was sixteen and his mom less than a year later.

It was just Sam and Isabel from that point on and they'd had no need for family drama. It had been enough to figure out how to survive. "Okay. Sure. What can I do to help?"

"Can I have you sit next to my mom during the ceremony? My aunt is several rows back and I convinced Lizzie, the receptionist from Eden's, to sit with her. Emma and I can worry about them during the reception."

Several guests filtered past, carrying elaborately wrapped gifts and chattering away.

"This isn't going to be a particularly fun affair for you, is it?"

"By the looks of it, no."

Sam couldn't help it. It was his inclination to help Mindy whenever she was in a tough spot.

"Okay, then. Introduce me to your mom."

Mindy took Sam's hand and they wound their way through the crowd gathered to enter the hotel's grand ballroom. They ducked past the ushers and marched straight down the aisle until they reached the first row.

"Sit right here." Mindy pointed to the second seat in. "My mom will be the first one down the aisle after the flower girls."

"Who's walking Sophie up the aisle?"

"Reginald. Eden's creative director."

"The guy who designs the window displays?"

Mindy nodded. "He was one of our gram's closest friends. He's like an uncle to us."

"The store really is an extended family, isn't it?"

"Of course it is. That's why I feel so guilty about it most of the time."

Sam studied the look of worry on Mindy's face. He knew very well her inner conflict over Eden's. She loved it, but she didn't like being tied down or told what to do. It would have been a very different situation if she'd chosen to work at Eden's. But she hadn't. Her inheritance had been tied to it. "Well, don't worry about me. I will have no problem taking care of your mom."

Mindy leaned down and kissed his cheek, leaving behind a tingle and probably lipstick, too. "You're the best. Thank you."

Sam took his seat. "You're more than welcome." He watched as Mindy walked away, her dress swooshing back and forth. She was easily the most complicated woman he'd ever had the pleasure to be with. He usually avoided complications. But there was something about Mindy that made them, at the very least, enticing.

Guests continued to file in and he took his chance to wave or nod at a few people he hadn't seen in some time. There was the Langford family, famous for their international telecom business—Adam and his wife, Melanie, and their twin boys. Adam's sister, Anna, and her financier husband, Jacob Lin, their little girl toddling between them. By the looks of Anna, there was another baby on the way. Joining them was Aiden, the oldest brother in the family, and his wife, Sarah, along with Aiden's young son.

The Locke family, owners of the hotel, were on hand, as well. Sawyer, the oldest, and his wife, PR whiz Kendall, along with their daughter. Noah, the youngest, and his wife, Lily. And real estate power couple Charlotte and her husband, Michael. Sam even got a glimpse of a few famous New Yorkers he'd never met, like British gin magnate Marcus Chambers and his wife, television personality Ashley George, better known as the Manhattan Matchmaker.

Soon enough, the guests had filled the ballroom. The processional music began. Along with everyone else, Sam stood and watched as two flower girls flung flower petals on the aisle runner and scurried to their parents as soon as they could. After that came Jill Eden, Mindy and Sophie's mom. She had the same flame-red hair as her daughters, but with a stylish streak of silver in the front, and carried herself as a woman who had known nothing less in her life than money and luxury. Sam pushed aside the thoughts of his own mom—they always seemed to creep in at moments like this, when major life events were occurring.

Jill smiled at Sam when she arrived at the first row. "You must be my wrangler. I've heard a lot about you." She held out her hand and raised an eyebrow, regarding Sam with suspicion. He was more than used to that treatment from members of the Eden family.

"I'm your honored guest. Nothing more than that."

"I have to hand it to my daughter. You're smooth. And handsome."

Sam stifled a grin as they returned their attention to the bridesmaids marching up the aisle. Even now he could see Mindy at the very end and he found his heart thumping harder. It all seemed a little silly. He wasn't the type to fall for the romanticism of an event like this, but there was something in the air—a warm feeling he couldn't put a name on. She smiled as she gracefully stepped her way past the guests, nodding and silently greeting people she knew. But then her sights landed on Sam, their eyes locked and he felt a verifiable jolt in the center of his chest. At any other time in his relationship with Mindy, this would have been par for the course. She had no trouble getting his engine revving. But he'd promised himself he wouldn't get caught up in her again, and this was the surest sign that he was doing exactly that. He forced himself to look down at his shoes. He'd gotten himself into this and he was going to have to find a way to get himself out.

"You must be very proud," Sam said, leaning

closer to Jill as Sophie made her slow march up the aisle on the arm of Reginald from Eden's.

She nodded. "I am. I just hope it lasts. My marriage was not a good one."

Sam found that an odd sentiment for the mother of the bride, but then again, Jill Eden had been burned by her husband, big-time.

"I should enjoy this while I can," she muttered out of the side of her mouth. "Sophie might be the only daughter I get to see married. Mindy's too independent. To her, it's a trap."

Sophie stopped at their row and gave her mom a kiss on the cheek. She ignored Sam, which was fine with him at this point. Then Reginald escorted her the final steps to the altar, where she took her place next to Jake. The officiant invited the guests to take their seats. Meanwhile, Jill's words about Mindy and her independence echoed in Sam's head. Mindy and Sam had never discussed marriage. In fact, the subject of commitment had never come up. Not that Sam had been particularly eager to go there, but he hadn't even had the chance to entertain it with her. It had always been Mindy who put up boundaries and set rules. She seemed to think that Sam had been entirely to blame in their many breakups, but the truth of their situation was that Mindy had always made the call. So perhaps her mother was right. Maybe Mindy saw all of this—

commitment and love—as nothing more than an ambush.

The ceremony went off without a hitch, and it was short and sweet, thank goodness. Sam spent most of the time studying Mindy, trying to resign himself to the fact that she would likely always be unfinished business in his life. He was the sort of the guy who either tied up loose ends or left them entirely behind. He suspected there would never be any winning with Mindy and not simply because he was still wary of being hurt. He couldn't imagine her ever letting him get close enough to try.

After Sophie and Jake exchanged their vows and said, "I do," the guests began to filter through a receiving line at the back of the room while hotel employees quickly moved the chairs and set things up for dinner. Not wanting to create tension with the bride and groom, Sam skipped the line and instead took his chance to exchange pleasantries with the various guests he'd most needed to reconnect with on a business basis. Thankfully, not a single person made a comment about Sam being a bit of an outcast with regard to the Eden family. Perhaps they had been discreet in their dislike for him.

Mindy and Sam were reunited when it came time for dinner and they were able to sit together, but there wasn't much opportunity for relaxed conversation. There were too many unpleasant undercurrents running through that room—Gerald shooting

Sam the evil eye, Jake and Sophie ignoring him, Jill downing drinks a little too fast and Mindy preoccupied with everything being perfect.

"The ceremony was nice," Sam said.

Mindy wiped her mouth with a napkin. "It was. We're almost at the finish line."

Sam hated the fact that she wasn't enjoying herself. He put his arm around her and leaned closer, speaking into her ear. "Relax. Everything is fine. Can I get you another drink?" Of course, Sam could do anything but relax right now, but he was fairly certain he was doing a good job of faking it. Being able to put his mouth so close to Mindy's neck wasn't helping him unwind. It only made his blood run a whole lot hotter. She not only looked stunning today, but he also had a real weakness for stressed-out Mindy. He knew how to unwind her. Again and again.

She turned her head toward his and kissed him on the cheek. "Gerald is watching us," she muttered.

"So I gathered." Sam didn't bother to look. He'd take Mindy's word for it. Instead, he took his chance to gaze deeply into her eyes, relishing the way they reflected uncertainty. She clearly had no idea what he would do next and how he loved the element of surprise. He leaned closer, and under the table, planted his hand on the top of her thigh, his fingertips just close enough to her center to send a message—he was hers for the taking. He placed a soft kiss on the corner of her mouth. Given the time and place, it was only a fraction of what he wanted to do, but he did make a point of being slow about it and allowing his lips to linger. It was chaste and sweet, when the thoughts running through his mind were of a more carnal variety. He wanted to pull her hair out of that neat twist, gather the gauzy fabric of her skirt in his hands and convince her to give in to him.

"You're so beautiful," he said.

"You're so bad." Mindy's eyelids fluttered and she showed him the most relaxed smile he'd seen from her all night.

Despite the need to keep Gerald at bay, Sam knew it wasn't good for him to be flirting with Mindy this way. The problem was, he no longer cared what was good for him. He only wanted whatever she did. "I'm only living up to expectations."

Sam was going to be the death of Mindy. Yes, they were putting on a show right now, but damn... It felt so real. It felt the way it had felt months ago, when things were fantastic between them, before they veered off course. His hand on her leg was one thing, but it was the kiss that really sent her into overdrive. It was enough to convince her that although they might eventually work as friends, for tonight, she needed more than that. She needed everything she'd wanted from him last night.

Unfortunately, that couldn't happen right now. Jake and Sophie were about to have their first dance. As the lights dimmed in the ballroom, Mindy took Sam's hand. "Come on. Let's go watch." She tapped her mom on the shoulder. "Mom. Join us. We'll be able to see better if we're up by the dance floor."

The three made their way closer to Jake and Sophie as the DJ told a few corny jokes and many more of the wedding guests followed their lead, joining them at the edge of the dance floor. There in the near dark, Mindy didn't hesitate to hold on to Sam's hand tightly. All she could think about was how glad she was to have him here. She couldn't imagine how little she would have enjoyed today if she'd had to do it all on her own.

Sophie and Jake looked so happy it was hard for Mindy to wrap her head around. She and Sophie had grown up with their parents' marriage as the only example of the way a couple should behave, and it had not been pretty. They had never been kind or sweet to each other. They only exchanged barbs and icy stares. Once Mindy and Sophie were old enough to have a better sense of what was going on in their parents' private lives, they quickly figured out that it wasn't just their father who was having many affairs. Their mother was plenty unfaithful. It was only last December, after Gram's will had been read and they learned that their cousin Emma was actually their half sister, that they also learned the most salient detail of the murky history of their parents' marriage. Their father's first affair had been Emma's mom, Aunt Jenny. The betrayal their mother felt over that would never go away, not even now, years after their father's death.

How Mindy hoped that Sophie and Jake would never reach that state with their marriage. She wanted to believe it wasn't preordained for their family. Sophie and Jake did genuinely love each other. That already gave them a leg up. Mindy wasn't certain that her parents had ever felt that way about each other. It was difficult to imagine how anyone would ever hurt someone they love so badly.

Sophie's and Jake's song wound down and the DJ invited the guests to join them. Mindy didn't even need to ask Sam if he wanted to dance… He was already leading her out onto the dance floor, his hand fully wrapped around her own.

She sucked in a sharp breath when he wound his arm around her waist and tugged her body against his. How she loved it when he took charge, but these were dangerous waters they were wading into. Every minute that ticked by seemed to be another tiny barrier breached—a touch, a warm breath, a kiss. She knew where that led with Sam… And he knew it, too. And she wasn't sure how they were going to handle their goodbye in a few hours, when the dances were done and it was time for her to go upstairs and for him to go home. Her sisters were sincere about the bet, and not just because they wanted to keep her at Eden's. They wanted to keep her from being hurt.

Reginald, in his pastel peach suit and one of his trademark plaid bow ties, and Mindy's mom joined the crowd on the dance floor, which made Mindy happy. She hadn't seen a smile on her mother's face in a long time. Sure, she was fairly certain she was drunk, but it didn't matter. Happiness was happiness. "It's nice to see my mom enjoying herself."

Sam glanced over at them. "I like your mom. She's different than I thought she would be."

"What do you mean by that?"

Sam shrugged. "She's not very sentimental. Most moms arc, especially if their daughter is getting married."

"Do you really think most moms are that way? I think of moms as being tough and pragmatic."

Sam cast Mindy a look that seemed to suggest she was off her rocker. "Yes, moms can be like that, but in general, I've found most moms to be tender-hearted. Especially when it comes to their children."

Mindy shook her head. "Yeah. That's not our mom. Is your mom like that?" Sam never, ever talked about his family.

Sam's lips formed a hard, thin line. "My mom passed away when I was in high school. But she was like that. Before she died."

"I'm so sorry. I had no idea. Why didn't you ever tell me this before?"

"It never came up."

"More like you failed to mention it. I've talked about my mom dozens of times around you. The subject definitely came up."

"I don't want to argue about it, Mindy. It's personal. And private. And something I don't enjoy discussing."

Mindy had to choke back several follow-up questions about Sam's mother. It was clear from his tone that he was very serious about this. Plus, her aunt Jenny was currently trying to cut in on her mom's dance with Reginald.

"Oh, crap," Mindy said. "This is exactly what I worried about."

Sam seemed to know exactly what Mindy was thinking as he twirled them closer.

"Have a seat," Jenny said. "I want to dance with Reginald."

"You're drunk," Mindy's mom snapped. "Go away."

"Ladies, ladies. There's more than enough of me to go around," Reginald said. He wasn't wrong. Tall, spindly and unavoidable in his colorful suit, it did feel as though he could easily make time for everyone.

Mindy glanced over at Sophie, who hadn't yet noticed the drama unfolding before them. "Aunt

Jenny, it's probably not the best time for dancing anyway. Sophie and Jake are about to cut the cake soon. We wouldn't want to miss that."

Aunt Jenny shot Mindy a look. "You're just like your mother. Bossy as hell. You can't tell me what to do." She closed her eyes and her head bobbed back and forth. Mindy knew for sure that her aunt had enjoyed a few too many glasses of champagne.

Mindy wanted to fight back, but this was all about de-escalation. "Um, I'm sorry. I'm just thinking about what Sophie would want. It's sort of my job as maid of honor."

Sam let go of Mindy and set his hand on Jenny's arm. "Ms. Stewart. I'm Sam Blackwell. I don't believe we've had the chance to meet. I'd be happy to walk you back to your table."

"I don't need your help!" Jenny shouted, yanking her hand back. The sound of her voice pierced all noise in the room, even the music. Everyone seemed to be staring at them.

Sophie and Jake let go of each other and started making their way through the crowd on the dance floor. Mindy's heart was about to pound its way through her chest. She had to do something, but what? There was no telling what Jenny might do if Mindy took the same approach Sam just had.

"Of course you don't need my help," Sam said, taking her hand and hooking it in the crook of his elbow. "I was merely offering to walk you there. Or perhaps we can head out to the lobby and get out of this stuffy ballroom."

Jenny's sights narrowed on Sam. "You're trying to get rid of me."

"Not at all. I only sense that maybe you're not enjoying yourself. We could go get a drink in the bar. You can tell me all about yourself."

Jenny was weaving again. "You're lucky you're so tall. I have a thing for ridiculously tall men."

"See? We make a perfect pair." Sam wasn't taking no for an answer. He began walking Jenny out of the ballroom and she had no choice but to stumble along.

Sophie appeared at Mindy's side. "What is he doing? Where is he taking her?"

"From the looks of it, he's saving your wedding reception."

"Oh, give me a break. Everyone's having a lovely time."

Mindy turned to her sister. "Would you like to bring back Aunt Jenny? Because I can gladly go get her."

Sophie pursed her lips. "No. I don't want that."

"Then I think we both know that Sam has done you a favor."

"That doesn't count for that much, Min. It'll take him a lifetime to make up for everything else he's ever done."

"I'm sure he's keenly aware of that. Now if you'll

excuse me, I'd like to at least go offer to be his backup." Mindy didn't wait for another comment from her sister and rushed through the ballroom doors, down the hall and out into the lobby. She spotted Sam and Jenny sitting at a side table with cups of coffee.

Sam subtly waved Mindy off, and so she hung back, watching him do this magic. Whatever he was saying, Jenny was clearly amused. She was warming up to him, smiling. Laughing, even. After a few moments, Sam beckoned one of the bell captains with a curl of his finger, gave him a tip and, before Mindy knew what was happening, Sam was walking Jenny outside. Mindy made her way across the lobby and peeked through the revolving doors just in time to see Sam put Jenny in a town car.

The look of victory on his face when he returned to the lobby was pure magic. It made Mindy's entire body tingle from head to toe. "Feeling pretty good about yourself, eh?" she asked.

"Shouldn't I be? I kept a bundle of dynamite from exploding in your sister's wedding reception. I'm pretty proud of myself, to be honest. I'm not usually that good at calming people down."

Mindy pulled him closer, drawing in his scent. It was even more intoxicating now than it had been out on the dance floor. His effect on her was more potent now, too. There were no prying eyes on them now. She felt free. "It's because you turned on the charm. Most women have no defense for that."

Sam's eyes darkened. "And what about you, Mindy? What are you keeping up your defenses for? We kept Gerald from asking you to dance. Your sister's wedding has gone off with only the most minor of hiccups. Looks to me like you're in the free and clear."

He was exactly right. She didn't need to be there for the cake cutting. She didn't need to worry any more about the bad things that might happen and her role in stopping any of them. She smoothed her hand over Sam's lapel and dared to look him square in the eye. "I think you're right. I think I can do whatever I want right now."

"And what is it that you want, Min?"

She bit down on her lower lip, a million ideas zipping through her head. Could she present Sam with a list of what she wanted? Because she certainly had enough material to make one. "Right now, with nobody watching us, I want to take you upstairs and get you out of this tux."

Five

The elevator door hadn't even closed before Mindy was kissing Sam, and he eagerly returned the favor. Lucky enough to be riding alone with him, Mindy saw no point in waiting, going straight for his tie and undoing the knot. She'd spent a lot of time and effort fighting this moment. It felt so good to simply give in to it. As she started to unbutton his shirt, she banished the little voice in her head that said this was just going to create problems. Problems were for tomorrow. Tonight, now that the weight of Sophie's wedding was gone, all she wanted was to get lost in Sam.

She flattened him against the wall, but he countered with a kiss that nearly blinded her. "I don't care that this is crazy. I want you." Her voice was a gasp, so desperate and breathless that it was as if it no longer belonged to her. She waited for Sam to respond, her chest heaving. She needed to hear him say that he needed her, too.

"Are you sure you want to do this, Min?" He reared back his head, leaving his mouth out of reach. At this point, even in heels, she would need a stepladder to kiss him. It felt mean and cruel, like he was showing off his masterful self-control. Mindy possessed so little of it when it came to him.

The elevator door slid open and she grabbed his hand, stealing down the hall to her room. "Am I sure I want to have sex with you? Yes. I didn't say that to be cute or coy." She waved her key in front of the lock and they were quickly inside. "Why? Are you not sure you want to have sex with me?" It felt like forever ticked by while she waited for his answer. She braced for the possibility that he would reject her. It was a mortifying prospect, but she could imagine him doing it. To get even. To have the upper hand.

Without a word, his hands went to her hips, which gave her a sliver of hope. She knew Sam. He wouldn't touch her if he didn't want her. "I'm sure I do. I just needed to ask."

Mindy was more than a little relieved. "Oh, good.

I was worried there for a minute." She sensed that wasn't enough of an answer. She did want him to know that the things he'd done for her over the last forty-eight hours had meant something. "Thank you for being such a sport about the wedding, and having to pretend to be my real date, and dealing with the moms. It really means a lot to me. Honestly, I don't know what I would have done without you." It was the truth. He was so much of the reason she'd found a way to enjoy herself.

"I'm not a bad guy. Maybe you can remember that the next time someone tries to convince you that I am."

Mindy really didn't want to get into this again. Such serious topics would ruin the impetuousness of the moment. She took his hands from her hips and walked backward, leading him farther into the room. "You know, Sam, right now it's just you and me and a beautiful bed. I don't think we should think about other people or let this go to waste." Mindy came to a stop when the backs of her legs hit the mattress.

Sam let go of her hands and rolled his shoulders out of his suit jacket, tossing it aside. He kicked off his shoes and took off his socks, then untucked his shirt, not taking his eyes off her. "The rest of my clothes are up to you."

Now they were getting somewhere. Mindy took her time unbuttoning his shirt, standing close to him and drawing in his warmth and masculine smell. She loved having his eyes on her as she spread her hands across his firm chest, using her fingers to trace the defined contours. She'd really missed seeing him without a shirt. She'd missed having her hands on his bare skin. If she were being honest, she'd simply missed being around him. His presence, when there were no outside forces between them, was comforting—like being wrapped up in a warm blanket. Paradoxically, being with him was also a thrill, causing her pulse to race and her head to swim.

He watched her as she unbuckled his belt, then unbuttoned and unzipped his pants, letting them drop to the floor. The look on his face, full of his unflinching restraint, made her that much more eager for the main event. She not only needed every inch of him, she wanted to put a smile on his face. Make him happy. Remind him that she was worth missing.

She wrapped one arm around his waist and, with her other hand, began to gently touch him through his boxer briefs. Her fingertips rode along his steely length, so tense she could feel how hard he was through the fabric. Sam groaned and closed his eyes, a mix of frustration and satisfaction crossing his face when she made it to the tip and rolled her thumb over the top, back and forth. She had no idea when this would happen again, if ever. There was too much standing between her and Sam. She wanted to enjoy every second of this.

"I have to sit," he mumbled. "You're making me dizzy." Sam slid onto the bed and leaned back on his elbows, his long body splayed out for her.

Mindy followed his cue and slipped his boxers down his hips. He was so magnificent it was hard to know where to look first. So she let her eyes rove over the landscape of his chiseled body, the long and muscled legs, his perfect abs, his sculpted shoulders. She wanted nothing between them and there was still a big something—her dress.

"I need to get out of this thing," she said.

"Yes, you do. I'll watch."

"I can't do the zipper on my own."

"Okay. Come here." He sat up and scooted to the edge of the bed.

She perched next to him and turned to provide access to the zipper. He first undid the clip in her hair and set it on the bedside table. He carefully uncoiled her hair from the twist, letting it fall down around her shoulders. She felt his presence, and not just his warmth, right behind her. His breaths were heavy, his heavenly smell swirling around her. He drew down the zipper, then peeled the dress away from her skin, blazing a trail of kisses along the channel of her naked back as he went. He had no idea what that did to her, the way it made the heat pool between her legs and the need double, then triple. She pulled the bodice forward and Sam reached around from behind, cupping her breasts in his hands, rolling her nipples between his fingers and pressing his chest against her back. She rolled her head to one side, relishing the jolts of electricity traveling between her breasts and her apex. It was as if her entire body had just come back to life. He kissed her neck with an open mouth, using his tongue, kneading her breasts and letting her get lost in the heavenly sensations. As amazing as it was, Mindy wanted more of him. She wanted to be able to see him. Kiss him.

She twisted her torso, then lay back on the bed, her dress still covering her from the waist down. Sam rose to his knees, hovering over her, then lowered his head, drawing her nipple into his mouth, swirling his tongue perfectly. He switched to her other breast and it was just as mind-blowing, especially when he would stop every few seconds and blow cool air against her overheated skin. He kissed the flat plane between her breasts, then dragged his mouth along her centerline. When he reached her waist, she wished her dress could just disappear.

Sam was on the case, though, standing and pulling the garment down her hips and tossing it away. He quickly kneeled on the floor in front of the bed and tugged her panties along the length of her legs, leaving her bare to him. He lifted one leg and placed it on his shoulder, then kissed his way along from the inside of her knee, down her inner thigh. Mindy's head rolled back when his lips found her apex and his tongue flicked at her center, then rolled in firm and steady circles. Sam had an incredibly talented mouth and he knew exactly how to please a woman. She wasn't sure if he was just good at reading her cues or if he just naturally knew what she liked. She only knew that he did.

Her head rocked back and forth over the silky bedding while her fingers massaged his scalp and combed through his thick hair. She was already heading toward her peak when he slipped a finger inside her, curled into her most sensitive spot. He was careful with her, and precise, staying homed in on the place that brought her the most pleasure. Mindy's mind was a blur of colors and blissful thoughts of Sam, and then the tension broke and she felt every muscle in her body go tight and let go, pulsing over and over again. He was unbelievable. And she intended to give him every bit of pleasure he'd just given to her.

Sam stretched out next to Mindy on the bed and kissed her softly. She quickly amped things up, hitching her leg over his hip and taking the kiss deeper, urging his tongue to coil with hers. He didn't need a single word of praise from her. She was telling him everything he wanted to hear with her actions as she rolled him to his back, kneeled between his legs and took his erection into her mouth.

That instant when her velvety tongue hit his skin made him lose all sense of time and place. How could one touch feel so impossibly good? She held him tightly between her lips, riding his length and rolling her tongue over the swollen head when she reached the tip. As good as it felt, he wasn't going to last long if she kept this up. That was a simple fact.

But he didn't even need to express it because Mindy did it first. "I love making you happy, but I really need to have you inside me."

My sentiments, exactly.

"I'm still on the pill, and I hate having to ask this question, but I need to know if you used a condom with any of the women you've dated since me."

"Believe it or not, it was only that one woman, and we didn't have sex."

Mindy sat back on her haunches. "You. Didn't have sex. With a woman."

He shook his head. "I swear."

Mindy cocked her head adorably, like one of those puppies with the big ears. Her gorgeous hair spilled over her shoulder. "I'm amazed."

He wasn't. He'd been there. He could explain the whole thing if needed. "Can we stop talking? I want you."

Mindy smiled and planted her hands on each side of his chest and her knees bracketed his hips. She leaned down into him, kissing him slowly. Softly. Like they were starting all over. It was a deliciously painful exercise in patience as her sumptuous lips glossed over his, and she put none of her body weight on him, hovering above him like a butterfly. From head to toe, he pulsed with need. Having only the softest brushes of her skin against his made it even more intense. Her breasts grazed his chest. Her nose nudged his cheek. Her knees squeezed his hips. His hands caressed the silky skin of her back, his fingers following the channel of her spine. But it wasn't enough. He needed her in a way he couldn't begin to describe.

He pulled her firmly against his chest and rolled her to her back, her red tresses splaying against the white bedding. She responded with a more intense kiss, one born of recklessness. It was the perfect reflection of the idea that they did not fit well into each other's lives, and yet they couldn't stay away from each other, no matter how hard they tried. He positioned himself at Mindy's entrance and drove inside, all while his mind spun out of control. Mindy gasped, then hummed with pleasure, a near mirror for everything going through his head. He hadn't forgotten how incredible she felt, but he had forgotten the magnitude of the moment when everything felt right and he couldn't have asked for another thing in the whole world.

Their bodies tumbled into a steady rhythm that suited them both perfectly. Mindy coiled her legs around his hips, pulling him closer, and he obliged, driving as deep as he could with every pass. She curled her fingernails into his back, the sting keeping him in the moment and heightening every sensation. Every muscle below his waist was contracting and releasing in an unceasing pattern. More intense. Closer to the brink. He listened to Mindy's breaths and moans, waiting for the moment when he got his body weight on just the right spot. Closer. And closer. And then he hit it. She tilted her hips and curled herself into him even more, holding on to him like she would never let go.

"I'm so close," Mindy mumbled into his neck. She kissed him fitfully, her mouth gaping.

Sam was so close it felt as if he was being teased by his own body. His peak was a whisper away but he focused on Mindy, rocking against her center and staying deep inside her. Her body pulled on his tightly and in a sudden rush, Mindy's head knocked back and she called out. Sam clamped his eyes shut and let his body take over, the climax rolling through him like a tsunami coming on shore. Over and over again, surges of warmth pushed him into contentment. A place where nothing else mattered but her.

He collapsed when the final waves washed over him. He rolled onto his back, right next to Mindy. He clasped his fingers around hers and raised her hand to his lips. He wasn't sure that this had been the smartest decision, but right now, he wasn't worried about being wise. He was too exhausted.

"Why does this always end up happening between us?" she asked.

He knew it wasn't a rhetorical question. It was real. And he also didn't know the answer aside from the obvious. "Because you're gorgeous and sexy and we have crazy chemistry?"

Mindy rolled onto her side and swished her hand across his chest. Even that mostly innocent touch threatened to get him going all over again. "You're sweet. I feel the same way about you. You're too enticing. I can't not kiss you. Which is sort of a problem, if you think about it."

Sam gave himself a minute to consider her answer. It didn't have to be a problem at all if she would stop letting her family come between them. There was a nagging sense deep inside him that there could be more between them than just sex. But he wasn't about to bring it up first. It had been hard enough to be rejected by her when she jettisoned him from her life. He was tough, but he wasn't impervious to pain. Plus, her mother had flat out told him exactly what he had suspected all along about Mindy—she needed her free will. The minute she started to feel trapped or obligated, she got panicky.

"Sam. I need to tell you something."

Sam couldn't begin to imagine what was coming next, but he feared she was about to do the thing he most dreaded—tell him to put his clothes on and leave. "Yeah. What?" If that was what she was about to do, it was best to get it over with. Maybe he'd finally learn his lesson this time.

"When I first told Sophie and Emma that I was bringing you to the wedding, they were concerned."

"They didn't understand that we struck a deal and you wanted to buy the Mercer from me?" Sam looked right at her as she pressed her lips together, waiting to answer his question.

"I didn't tell them that part. I worried that Sophie would think it was uncool that I was essentially leveraging my plus-one to her wedding. Plus, I didn't want her to question your motives. I figured it was good enough that they thought I had asked you because I was trying to keep Gerald away."

"Something tells me you would have had no problem dealing with him."

"Maybe. Probably. He was more of an annoyance than anything, but that's not what I'm trying to tell you. I'm trying to tell you that Sophie and

Emma were worried that I was going to fall under your spell."

Sam laughed. He couldn't help it. "I have a spell? I had no idea."

"Oh, you do. You definitely do. You make me a little bit crazy, Sam."

He reached out and cupped her bare shoulder, trailing his fingers down her arm. "Mindy, sweetheart, I'm pretty sure you're crazy on your own. It's not my fault if I bring it out in you."

Mindy swatted his chest. "Hey. Let me finish." She then closed her eyes tight and scrunched up her face. "This is so stupid. I'm not even sure I can say it out loud."

"What?"

"My sisters and I made a bet. We made a bet that I won't fall for you again. If I do, if I get involved with you, I have to stay at Eden's for an extra year. Which obviously I don't want to do."

There was a lot about this that Sam needed to unpack. It might take him hours to sort this out in his head. "Again? Does that mean you fell for me before?"

Mindy unleashed a groan. "Well, yeah, but you had to have known that."

Sam shrugged. "How could I have possibly known that?"

"Don't guys always know when a woman is gaga over him?"

"Gaga? No. I knew you liked me enough to sleep with me. That was about it."

"Well, it's not like I even had the slightest idea how you felt about me. Everything always felt so temporary. You were always coming into town, then leaving again. It was hard to watch you go."

If she thought it was hard to watch him go, she needed to know what it felt like to be asked to leave. Sam realized just how little time he and Mindy had spent talking about anything of substance when they'd been together before. They'd given in to the physical side of their attraction, but they hadn't bothered to explore anything deeper. He'd always assumed that was what Mindy wanted. Now he was starting to wonder if he'd been wrong. Under any other circumstances, this revelation could have made this the perfect time to wade into those deeper waters, but the bet with her sisters made everything infinitely more complicated.

"How serious do you think Sophie and Emma are about the bet?"

"Dead serious. They don't want me to get hurt and they don't want me to leave the store."

"So why did you take it in the first place?"

Mindy sat up and pushed away, distancing herself from him and resting her back against the headboard. "It was supposed to be insurance. I was trying to protect myself."

"From me?" He knew he'd done things that had

been construed as bad, but he'd never had anything less than Mindy's best interests at heart.

"More like from my weakness for you."

Six

In the breaking light of day, Mindy felt Sam's presence in her hotel room, and with that came the worry. Had she made a mistake? Had last night been a grave error? She didn't want to think so. She and Sam worked well together, at least for short stretches. Last night had been an amazing one and her thirst for him wasn't nearly quenched.

From the other side of the bed, he stirred. He'd be awake soon, which meant he'd be leaving. He never stayed for long. Her sister Sophie was off to the airport for her honeymoon in Bali later that day. Her sister Emma was also about to embark on a romantic getaway—a trip to England to visit

Daniel's parents. Mindy, however, would be returning to work. Yes, she loved staying busy and being productive, but where was her fun? Why couldn't she have a love life like her sisters did?

It would be easy to blame her drive and determination. She'd always had a need to succeed, and that had gotten in the way of love many times. Had it gotten in the way with Sam? If so, the bet made things even messier. If she lost the bet, she would be stuck at Eden's for an extra year. Sophie would never let her off the hook, in part because she was so set on having Mindy on board at the store forever.

Sam wrapped his arm around Mindy's waist. He pressed his long body against hers, his heat pouring into her. She loved these moments together, when it was just the two of them, and all in their world was relatively calm. When everyone else wasn't weighing in on her choices. Sam nuzzled the back of her neck with his nose and pressed a soft kiss against her nape. She closed her eyes and inhaled deeply, relishing every second of this moment. It would be gone soon. Quite possibly gone forever. However complicated, Sam was an amazing man. There were only so many times she could shoo him away before some smart woman, somewhere, would keep him around.

But maybe Mindy could have some more of this

blissful feeling with Sam, at least for another week, while her sisters and their watchful eyes were away.

Mindy rolled to her other side and faced Sam. "Hey, handsome. You awake?" she whispered.

He nodded, his eyes still closed. "Getting there."

"Can I ask you a question?"

"You just did."

"Okay, fine, funny guy. What do you have going on this week?"

He cleared his throat and their bodies pressed against each other again. "The usual. There's a bull-headed woman who wants to buy a building from me. I guess I need to follow through on that one, huh?"

Mindy smiled and settled her face in his neck. "I do plan on holding you to that. I wasn't kidding when I said I wanted that building."

"Oh, believe me. I know. Any time I know what you want, I don't let it go. You can be very difficult to figure out."

Mindy didn't see herself that way at all. "I'm so easy to figure out, it's ridiculous."

"Then I must be spectacularly stupid."

"What's that supposed to mean?"

"Any time I ever think I'm doing right by you, I end up falling flat on my face. I ended up kicked out of your life."

"But we're talking about big missteps, Sam. Interfering with Eden's. Leaking information about Emma to the press."

"Both done at times when you were deeply unhappy and I was trying to find a way to turn that around."

Had his actions really been so secretly benevolent? Mindy still had her doubts.

"Sam, what happened with you and Jake?"

He drew a deep breath through his nose. "I'd call it a misunderstanding. He thought we were full partners, but I didn't see us that way. I felt that we were helping each other out. It's just something people do to get by, right? Especially when you're starting out?"

"I don't understand why he would feel so betrayed by that. He's clearly still holding a major grudge."

"I made a lot of money with the deal he thought I'd cut him in on. Money makes grudges stick."

"So why didn't you include him?"

Sam took another breath and rolled to his back, away from her. She missed him the instant he was gone, in part because she sensed his anger bubbling to the surface. "I needed the money. Not for myself, but for someone else. And for a good reason. So I did it. If I had cut Jake into the deal, I wouldn't have made enough money to take care of the problem."

From the tone of Sam's voice, Mindy could only infer that he preferred this to be the end of the subject, but she didn't want it to be. She wanted to know more. If he was ever to be redeemed in the eyes of her family, she had to know the truth. "If you were helping someone, why didn't you just tell him that?"

"Because it's none of his business. This was personal and although we were friends, this wasn't something I wanted to share with anyone." Sam's voice now had an edge of agitation that Mindy had never heard. He threw back the covers and climbed out of bed.

"Where are you going?"

"I'm getting dressed. I'm leaving."

"Wait. Don't. Don't go."

He stood before her, naked, every inch of his stunning body on display. "I don't want to play this game anymore, Mindy. It's not fun and I have the distinct impression that I'm always going to lose. I don't like to lose. Ever."

Mindy sat up and scooted to the edge of the bed, clutching the sheet to her chest. She couldn't sit before him feeling so exposed. "I don't think it's unfair of me to question you on certain things."

"But you do nothing but question me, Mindy. My motives. My tactics. The things I say. It's exhausting. You know, you and I got along perfectly until you started talking to Sophie and Jake. Nothing has been the same since then. I live under a cloud of suspicion and I can't take it."

Mindy couldn't begin to form a response. There were too many thoughts whirring around in her brain. He was right about Sophie and Jake. She hadn't formed her opinion of Sam fully independent of others. And that certainly wasn't fair. She wouldn't like it if someone had done that to her. "You're right. I need to take the things you say for what they are and stop reading into them. If you tell me that you believe you had no choice but to cut Jake out of that deal all those years ago, I believe you."

Sam arched both eyebrows and lowered his chin. Even in the soft early-morning light, she could see exactly how skeptical he was of her. "That doesn't change the fact that you made a bet with your sisters that you wouldn't fall into my clutches. Whatever you may think of me, Mindy, I'm not a spider waiting for its prey to make a fatal error."

Mindy exhaled, a bit exasperated. He was right again. It was only a fear of her own weakness that had made her take the bet in the first place. She couldn't blame Sam for it. "The bet was stupid. I never should have agreed to it." It was especially pointless since the entire aim had been for Mindy to force herself to stay away from Sam. Judging by the state of the bed, she had failed spectacularly. If Sophie knew what happened last night, she would already have Mindy on the hook for another year.

Sisterly guilt goes far. "But I'm stuck in it. Sophie will never let me out."

"Well, think of it this way. At least you know she wants you close. That counts for something." He knocked his head to one side and folded his arms across his chest. "From where I sit, it counts for quite a lot."

"I want *you* close." Mindy could hardly believe she'd had the nerve to say it. Even she marveled at the conviction with which she'd uttered the words.

"I love morning sex as much as anyone, but maybe we need to stop doing this. Last night was incredible, but I can't take everything that goes with it."

Mindy carefully peeled back the covers and stood, facing him, taking the zaps of electricity that pinged back and forth between them. "I'm serious, Sam. I do want you close. The last few months have been miserable. And I want a chance to spend time with you again like we did at the beginning, out from under the microscope of my family."

"What are you suggesting?"

"Sophie's out of the country for a week. So is Emma." She took his hands in hers, rubbing her thumbs back and forth across his knuckles. "Let's use this time to be together."

Sam nodded slowly, but she knew he wasn't agreeing to this—he was thinking. By the dark look in his eyes, it was difficult for him to reach a decision. "Then what? After the week?"

That was the question she'd feared most, but she owed him an answer. "If we still like each other after a week, I'll go to my sisters and try to work out a compromise."

He shook his head. "I'm not a compromise. I refuse to be one. Either you tell them we're together because we are, or we aren't."

Mindy was more than a little taken aback. It wasn't like Sam to draw such a hard line in the sand. But she'd backed herself into a corner here and she had to keep her eye on the prize—she wanted to give Sam yet another chance. "Okay. It's a deal."

"And we stay at my apartment. Not yours."

"I wasn't aware you were in a position to make demands."

"Those are my rules. You've never even been to my apartment."

"Did you ever invite me over?"

"I did. Many times."

After their long and meaty conversation, Sam headed back to his apartment to prepare for Mindy's arrival that afternoon. He had never before cohabited with a woman, and although this was only for a week, it did make him unsettled. His place was his retreat. He'd purposely bought in Tribeca and avoided the social posturing of Central Park or the

Upper East Side, where Mindy lived. Of course, his neighborhood was the most expensive in the city at the moment and one of the trendiest, but at least he felt as though he was mingling with people who'd made their money and were enjoying it, rather than acting as though they were made of it.

His apartment occupied the top two floors of a renovated warehouse. There were exposed brick walls, tall arched lead-paned windows and beautifully restored hardwood floors. The kitchen was a showpiece, with white marble countertops, an industrial range and espresso-brown custom cabinetry. His favorite part of the apartment was the library, perched on an elevated platform circling his entire living room, with his home office occupying one corner. There were thousands of books, many original editions, and several places to curl up and get lost in a good read. He spent more time in that part of the house than any other, and he used his time before Mindy's arrival to unwind in his favorite chair, a chocolate-brown antiqued leather recliner, with a good mystery.

He was so immersed in the story that he jumped when his cell phone rang. He fished it out of his pocket and consulted the caller ID. He'd thought perhaps it was Mindy, but it was his sister, Isabel. "So you finally call me back," he answered. "I was beginning to worry."

"I know. I know. Work is crazy. What can I say?"

"You can say that you're sorry. You can say that you won't wait more than an entire week to call me back next time. I do worry, you know."

"About me?" Isabel laughed. "I'm the oldest. It's my job to worry about you."

"Somehow I don't think that applies anymore now that we're both in our midthirties."

"Unfortunately, I'm more like late thirties. And you'll always be my little twerp of a brother. I don't care if you are six foot six. It'll always be like that. No matter what you do."

Sam laughed and set his book on the side table next to his chair. He didn't know what he would do without his sister in his life. She was not only a rock, she shared his past. It was so nice to be able to talk to someone without having to skirt topics. It was so much easier to just be completely open about everything. "I guess I should let you know why I called," he said.

"Whatever works. I'm fine with just catching up, too."

"I got a call from the woman who runs the fundraisers for ALS research. You know I make at least one major contribution every year. Anonymously."

"Of course. Mr. Secretive has to keep things under wraps."

"Hey. That's not fair. It's just a lot easier for me from a business perspective if people don't know about my involvement with the charity. I don't need anyone's pity."

"I've heard this story from you before."

Sam grumbled under his breath. "Anyway, they need a new sponsor and host for this year's gala. They found themselves in a precarious situation. The original hosts were Senator Miles and her husband. That's not the best optics right now."

"Ouch. Yeah. A big public sex scandal doesn't really sell charity fundraiser tickets, does it?"

"No. It does not."

"And you're hesitating because you don't want to deal with putting your name on the event."

"I'd also have to make a speech and get people to open up their checkbooks. That means telling a sad story. That means talking about Mom in front of a room of hundreds of people, many of whom I would like to be able to do business with."

Isabel sighed. "That does sound like a lot to deal with."

"They keep calling me about it and I haven't given them an answer. I need to decide soon. I don't want to be the reason they get held up."

"Well, let me say this. First off, nobody in that room is going to be anything less than sympathetic to what happened to Mom. And it might help people see a softer side of you. You do have a bit of a reputation. We've talked about this before."

"Yes. I know." Sam shifted in his seat and

crossed his legs, feeling surprisingly uncomfortable in his favorite chair. "And you also know that there are details surrounding Mom's death that don't reflect well on Dad. Or could create a scandal if they ever came out. I don't want to give anyone an excuse to dig."

"That was nearly twenty years ago at this point. And I don't think there's anything that anyone could find out. Dad's accident was found to be exactly that. The insurance company and the police both did a thorough investigation and reached the same conclusion. You took care of the whole thing later. You destroyed the note he left. I mean, you and I will always know what really happened, but nobody else ever will."

Sam drew a deep breath through his nose. "I suppose you're right. It still worries me. I just…" Sam had to choke back a surprising lump of emotion. "I would never want anyone to ever speak ill of him. He did everything for us."

"I know, honey. I know."

Sam closed his eyes and willed his bad memories away. Still it was hard to do—there were so many images permanently emblazoned in his mind. Especially the note. He might have burned it, but it would always live on in his head. He could still see his dad's chicken-scratch handwriting, the way the words became more difficult to read as it went on about the reasons why he'd decided to do the unthinkable. "So you think I should do this? Is that what you're saying?"

"I do think you should do it. I think you will feel good about it when it's done. I think it will ultimately be a good thing when it comes to your business. It might even bring you some new opportunities. And most important, it'll give me an excuse to come to New York and brag about my little twerp of a brother."

Sam couldn't help but be excited by the prospect of seeing Isabel. It didn't happen nearly enough. "That would be amazing. I'd love to have you here. For moral support, if nothing else." He started to realize exactly how much of an undertaking this would be. He would be expected to bring in ticket sales, and, of course, there was the matter of the speech.

"I wouldn't miss it. I promise to be there, looking amazing, and clapping louder than anyone for you."

He breathed a sigh of relief. This would be a lot of work, but at least he'd made a decision. That part didn't need to weigh on him anymore. "You sure you'll be able to get away from work?" Isabel was a high-powered attorney in Washington, DC. She was also a bit of a fixer. If an important person got in trouble and needed a discreet way out, she was there, for a price.

"Yes. I'm sure. Honestly, I need to take a few days off anyway and I'd love to spend some time in New York. I'm so tired of DC. There are far too many politicians here."

"Aren't they your bread and butter?"

"Annoyingly so. I'd rather just get back to working with regular rich people. They're far more interesting and far less predictable."

"Maybe you should think about moving here. It is your firm, after all."

"Funny that you should mention it. I've been thinking about exactly that for a while now. It would be nice if you and I lived in the same place again. We haven't done that since we were kids."

"It would be amazing."

"Plus, I need to find a man. I think I've already exhausted the dating pool here."

"I'm surprised you have time."

Isabel laughed. "Oh, honey, I make time."

Sam closed his eyes and shook his head. "And I do not need to know anything more than that."

"What about you? Anyone new since the few women you dated after Mindy Eden stomped all over your heart?"

Sam had confided in his sister about Mindy. Not everything. Just basic venting. Isabel was his only personal confidante, unless you counted Mindy, and they had only ever skimmed the surface. He knew he was going to catch some crap for having Mindy back in his life, but he also knew he couldn't hide it. There were likely stories about Sophie's wedding in the tabloids today. At the very least, the rumor mill was always running. "Yeah. About that. I, uh, went to Mindy's sister's wedding yesterday. I went as Mindy's date, actually. Well, it was more of a business arrangement, I guess." With every passing word, Sam realized just how convoluted his situation with Mindy was. There was no putting a label on it. He couldn't even explain it to his own sister.

"Have you seriously let her back into your life? You already know I'm not a fan."

Sam couldn't hide anything from Isabel. "We had a really good time together at the wedding. And, well, we've decided to spend some time together on a trial basis. We'll see how it goes."

Isabel did not respond to that bit of information.

"I can hear you breathing," Sam said.

"I'm thinking. About how badly I want to lecture you. And whether or not it's worth it to get on a plane and read you the riot act in person."

"Save it. I love you, but I can handle this. If nothing else, I feel like Mindy and I have unfinished business. Hopefully this will at least give me a chance to have some closure."

"Closure is a myth. Like unicorns and leprechauns. Closure is just a word for learning to ignore pain."

Was Isabel right? Was Sam putting his heart on the line for all the wrong reasons? His phone beeped with a text and he pulled it away from his ear to see the message.

I'm here.

He couldn't help it—his heart rate picked up at the idea that Mindy had arrived.

"Hey, Is. I have to go."

"Okay. Keep me posted on the Mindy Eden situation. And send me the link to buy tickets for the fundraiser."

"Will do. Love you."

"I love you, too."

Sam hung up and raced down to his door to let Mindy in. Her driver was unloading the back cargo area, setting three…four…five suitcases on the sidewalk. "Wow. You came prepared."

Mindy peered up at him from behind oversize Jackie O sunglasses. She cracked a dazzling smile. "A week for me is like a month for anyone else."

Sam had more than a passing thought that at least with this much stuff, it would be harder for her to run out the door. At the very least, it would slow her down. He took two of the bags, Mindy wheeled one, her driver the rest, and Sam led them to the elevator.

"I can take everything from here," Sam said to her driver.

"You sure, Mr. Blackwell? I'm happy to ride up," Mindy's driver said.

The reality was that Sam was too eager to finally have Mindy all to himself. He didn't want to wait. "I'm sure. I'll take it from here." He held the elevator open by leaning into it and reached into his wallet for a twenty, hoping a tip might encourage him to go.

The driver waved it off. "Oh, no sir. Thank you. I'm just fine."

Mindy turned to him. "Pick me up outside at eight tomorrow morning for work?"

"You got it, Ms. Eden. Have a nice night." With that, the driver departed.

Sam stepped on board, punched in his access code, and they rode to his main floor. He let her go first, then quickly offloaded her bags. Now, finally, he and Mindy were alone in his apartment. And he wasn't quite sure where to start. Their usual routine was to start taking off each other's clothes, and he certainly hoped that would happen at some point. But there was another part of him that was hoping he and Mindy could start breaking a few old habits. Perhaps they could finally get down to a different kind of business…the one where a man and a woman learn how to be friends.

"Your apartment is stunning," Mindy offered, walking through the foyer and into the open living room. Sam rarely had visitors, so it was fun to watch as her eyes were immediately drawn up. "Ooh. What's up there? A library?"

"My favorite part of the house. Can I show you?"

"Yes. I can't wait to see it."

Sam took her hand and led the way past his sectional sofas and fireplace, to the far side of the room, and up the modern wrought-iron staircase to the loft.

When they arrived up there, Mindy ran her hands across the spines of the leather-bound volumes. "I had no idea you were such a reader."

"I can spend hours up here. Days. It's my escape."

She turned to him, her perfume wafting gently to his nose and wrapping around him like an embrace. Having her here made everything different—the air was charged with something warm he couldn't describe. "Do you feel like you need an escape?" she asked.

"I did when I was a kid. I guess I just got in the habit." Panic overtook him as he realized he'd opened himself up to questions about his childhood. He wanted to open up to Mindy, but not about that. Not yet. "What's your escape, Mindy?"

"Judging by the number of suitcases I brought, it looks like you are."

Seven

It took less than twenty-four hours for Mindy to feel at home with Sam. They'd spent their Sunday afternoon and evening in and out of bed, enjoying each other's company in ways that left Mindy so relaxed, she'd never felt more prepared to tackle her Monday and the rest of the workweek. They'd had dinner in, which Mindy had prepared, while Sam was in charge of pouring wine and distracting her with his hands on her hips and his lips on the crook of her neck. They'd stayed up late, bodies twined under the covers, watching old movies. Mindy learned that Sam not only had a penchant for books, but he knew quite a lot about film, as well. She cherished the chance to learn these new things about him, little details that helped to color in her sense of who he was.

Things were certainly different being at Sam's place as opposed to her apartment, and Mindy couldn't help but wonder if it was about more than a change of location. They were still keeping things secretive as they'd had to do many times before, but there was a sense of freedom that hadn't been there before. Sophie and Emma were far away. There were no prying eyes watching over her, questioning her time with Sam and making her second-guess herself at every turn.

Now that it was Monday morning, and this would be Mindy's first time running Eden's on her own, it was time to see if this newfound freedom extended to her work life, as well. Mindy's driver, Clay, was waiting for her outside Sam's apartment right on time, and Sam walked her out to the curb to say goodbye. It was another gorgeous fall day. The sun was strong, the sky clear, and the air crackled with autumn crispness. "I guess it's time for me to head in," Mindy said, peering up into Sam's face.

His arms circled her waist, pulling her closer. She loved the way he always sought this physical closeness. It was more than hot—it made her feel wanted. Needed. "Before you go, do you think you can get away for a few hours at lunchtime?"

Mindy smoothed her hand over the lapel of Sam's jacket. "What did you have in mind? Meet back here?" She and Sam had just spent a good half hour in the shower together. The memory of his soapy hands all over her body sent a zip of excitement along her spine. Still, she was amazed that his mind was already back on sex. Apparently he was just as determined as she was for them to squeeze as much into their week together as possible.

"Actually, it's a surprise. I'll pick you up at Eden's? One o'clock?"

This put Mindy in a bit of an awkward situation. If he was at the store, people would see him. But she also knew that the employees were not prone to gossip, and with Sophie and Emma in far-flung corners of the globe, she decided it was a chance she could live with. "Sounds great. I can't wait." She kissed him on the lips and he stole the chance to squeeze her backside with one of his massive hands. She mentally pinched herself, feeling incredibly lucky.

Clay got her to the store much faster than she ever arrived from her place on the Upper East Side—another unexpected bonus of staying with Sam. The morning went smoothly—a meeting with the department heads, a conference call about a new exclusive designer the store was courting and a preliminary chat with Reginald about the store's Christmas displays, especially the world-famous windows. Sophie, the self-appointed duchess of all things Christmas at Eden's, would be brought in later. Reginald merely wanted to run a few ideas by Mindy. She was "far less picky," as he put it.

With about a half hour before Sam was to arrive, Mindy switched to some BMO emails, and that was where her day became decidedly complicated. There had been endless internal strife lately, and it seemed to be getting worse rather than better. There were arguments over creative directions, battles over production schedules and dismal reports from the finance department about supply costs. The company had been firing on all cylinders a year ago and now they were barely keeping their collective head above water.

She shot off an email to acting CEO Matthew, offering suggestions as to how to fix their problems, and asking him to give her an update on everything. She didn't want to micromanage him, but she did want him to take some ownership of the situation and stop letting her employees argue with each other forever. She was tempted to call a staff meeting and give everyone a pep talk about cooperation and teamwork, but she didn't want to undermine Matthew. If this was going to work, he had to appear to be in charge. Still, it made her that much more eager to get out of Eden's and back to running BMO. Fourteen months was all she had left. Of course, there was the bet to worry about, but right now, that was a fleeting thought. It was easy to ignore without Sophie and Emma exerting their sisterly pressure.

Five minutes before Sam was due to arrive, Mindy shut down her laptop, grabbed her Birkin bag and ducked into the ladies' room to freshen up. Her hand trembled a bit as she reapplied her lipstick. She couldn't help but be excited by the notion of Sam surprising her. What did he have up his sleeve? A fancy lunch? Shopping trip? With the city at their feet, the possibilities were endless.

Mindy emerged from the bathroom and Lizzie flagged her down from reception. "Ms. Eden, there's a man on the phone named Benjamin Summers. He asked to speak to either you, Sophie or Emma. He said he's calling about a promissory note. Something about a loan your grandmother took out?"

"I have no idea who that is. Is he from a bank?" Mindy hooked her bag on her arm and walked over to Lizzie's desk.

Lizzie shook her head. "He wouldn't tell me where he was calling from. He only gave his name."

"Sounds like a scam to me." Ever since Gram had passed away, there had been countless people attempting to get their hands on Eden's in any number of ways.

"That's what I was thinking. What would you like me to do?"

"I guess you should take a message, but between you and me, I'm not going to call him back."

Behind Mindy, the elevator dinged. Mindy's heart did a flip in her chest and she whipped around only to see Sam step through the doors. There was something about that moment when he walked into the room—everything around her became fuzzy, and he was the only thing in focus.

"Lizzie, I'm headed out to lunch." Mindy turned for a second, catching that "good for you" look in Lizzie's eye. "I might be gone a few hours."

"No worries, Ms. Eden. We'll hold down the fort."

"Ready?" Sam asked.

"Absolutely."

Mindy's escape was perfect. Everyone else in the executive offices was at lunch and Lizzie would never breathe a word of this to anyone. Mindy was the one who'd gotten her the biggest raise she'd ever received. Not that she didn't deserve it—she absolutely did. She put up with the three sisters and their constant drama, and never let it faze her.

As soon as they were alone in the elevator, Mindy took Sam's hand. "Where are we going?"

"I told you. It's a surprise."

She couldn't have hidden her smile if she'd

wanted to. This made her happy. Normal relationship stuff. Could she and Sam have that? Could she talk Sophie and Emma out of the silly bet? If her week with Sam continued like this, Mindy was going to have to sit her sisters down and explain to them that they were going to have to put her happiness before the things that they wanted.

Mindy and Sam were soon in the back of Sam's black stretch SUV with his driver at the helm. They'd traveled only a few blocks west from Eden's Thirty-Sixth Street entrance before it became apparent where they were headed—the Lincoln Tunnel. "We're going to New Jersey?" she asked.

"I should have blindfolded you," Sam quipped.

Mindy was momentarily distracted by the idea. "Wait. Are we going to see the Mercer?"

Sam reached down for his black leather messenger bag and produced a thick envelope, which he handed to her. "Here you go. The purchase agreement."

"Seriously? You got it done already?" Mindy took the packet from him, hearing the excitement in her own voice. So many of the problems with BMO could be solved with the purchase of this building. Every issue she'd had to grapple with that morning would improve simply by having her entire operation in one place.

"Of course I got it done already. A promise is a

promise." He gestured at the envelope with a nod. "Go ahead. Read it."

"Right." She unhooked the metal clasp and pulled out the sheaf of papers. "Of course, I'll have to wait to sign it until I have my lawyer look at it." Everything between Sam and her was going so well, but surely he understood that this was business. "You get it, right? I have to make sure everything is in order."

"Absolutely I understand."

She was glad that it didn't feel as though there was any subtext in his answer, one of her not trusting him. She began to look through the pages, skimming the key points and clauses, until she reached the section with the purchase price. She nearly passed out when she saw the number. "A dollar?" Mindy had no idea her own voice could reach such a ridiculously high pitch. "You're selling me the building for a dollar? Seriously? Is this a joke?"

Sam frowned, which made Mindy feel horrible. "I wanted to do something nice for you. Something sort of romantic." His response was adorably tentative. Sam was always so self-assured, it was humbling to see this hint of vulnerability.

"Flowers are romantic. A building that could save my entire mess of a business? I don't even know what to say, Sam. This is beyond romantic. It's so generous of you. I don't know if I can accept this. It's such a huge gift." She set the papers down on the seat between them and took his hand. "It's seriously the nicest thing I think anyone has ever done for me. Thank you." She leaned over and gave him a soft and sensuous kiss. She wanted him to know that she truly appreciated the sweet gesture.

"You're welcome. I'm just happy that you're happy. Seeing that look on your face is all the reward I need."

"I'm curious why you did this, though. Is there something you want or need?"

"I don't need anything more than you right now, Mindy."

Mindy's heart fluttered so fast it made it feel as though she might float away. She was seriously starting to feel light-headed from Sam's brand of romanticism, but the driver turned into the drive for the Mercer and this was no time for letting her head stay in the clouds. She peered out the window to look at the building she hadn't seen in over a month. An old sugar processing plant, the Mercer had character for days—five floors clad in red brick with sky-high factory windows and a hint of art deco architecture. It was going to be a real showstopper once she turned it into everything they needed it to be. "I can't believe this is going to be mine. Everything under one roof. It's amazing."

Sam's driver parked the car and they climbed

out. That was when Sam unveiled his second surprise of the day. His driver had a blanket and picnic basket in the front seat with him. "We shouldn't be much more than an hour," Sam said, taking the items from him and closing the door.

"A picnic? You are full of surprises."

"I want us to enjoy our week, and this is part of that. Plus, a businesswoman's got to eat, right?"

"I am slightly starving. So yes."

He took Mindy's hand and led her around back to the door next to the loading dock bays. He unlocked it and presented the key to her. "You should probably be in charge of this. It's your building."

"I haven't even signed the contract yet. How do you know I'm good for that dollar?"

He bounced his eyebrows up and down and they stepped inside. "Something tells me I'll get it out of you one way or another."

The main floor was a cavernous, empty space with the building's highest ceilings—twenty-two feet. "This is where all of the shipping and fulfillment will go," Mindy said. In her mind, she could see her employees packing boxes with wedding invitations, birth announcements or Christmas cards. The idea filled her with hope, something she hadn't been feeling about BMO in recent weeks.

"Sounds perfect," Sam said as they walked over to the back stairs. "I guess we'll have to hoof it."

"No electricity, no elevator."

They carefully ascended the five flights, which were dimly lit right now, narrow beams of sunlight filtering through windows that needed a good wash. Still, Mindy was struck with the feeling that things were turning around. She hadn't worried that Sam would go back on his promise to sell her the building, but she'd certainly never expected him to sell it to her for a song. More than anything, she'd never imagined he would take something so important, yet decidedly *not* romantic—an old factory—and turn it into such a sweet and sentimental outing. He knew exactly how much this meant to her and he'd gone the extra mile to make it special.

"I scouted out the perfect location for our picnic. Up here, fifth floor." Sam pulled open the heavy metal door at the top of the final landing, which creaked loudly on its hinges. "Ladies first."

Mindy blinked several times while her eyes adjusted to all of the light. The sun positively poured through the windows lining the straight shot of what would eventually be the executive floor. "It looks like somebody cleaned up here." Mindy turned and took it all in. This was not what it had looked like when she and Matthew had walked the space before making an offer. The windowpanes were crystal clear. The original wide-plank hardwood floors weren't covered in dust and dirt like they had been downstairs.

"I knew we were going to have lunch. I didn't

want you to get whatever you were wearing all dirty," Sam said.

"When did you have time to plan all of this? Or even have it done? It must have taken days."

One corner of Sam's mouth turned up and Mindy saw something she'd never seen on his face—a blush in his cheeks. "It took about a week."

She had been staying at Sam's apartment for only a day. It had only been yesterday morning that they'd decided to try at all. "You planned this before the wedding? Back when we were keeping things platonic and focused on being friends?"

"Well, yeah. I like doing nice things for you, but I know I haven't done a great job of it in the past. Plus, I know how much this means to you. I hear it in your voice. I see it in the way your eyes blaze when you talk about it. Not many people have a vision. Not many people are capable of being passionate about what they do. I wanted to reward that. It's not something you see every day."

Mindy gazed up at Sam, overwhelmed with a feeling she never flirted with—love. Did she love him? Was that what this was? She was certain she was at least falling under Sam's spell again, this time harder than all of the others put together. Could she have the happy ending her sisters had managed to get for themselves? Or was she once again allowing herself to be swept away by the handsome man with the inexplicable pull on her?

* * *

Sam hoped he hadn't overstepped. The look on Mindy's face was hard to decipher—he'd expected smiles, not sadness, and certainly not a tear rolling down her cheek. Before he could ask if she was okay, she flung her arms around him.

"Thank you so much. I don't even know how to express how much this means to me."

He set the picnic basket down on the ground and took his chance to wrap his arms around her. "Any idiot could figure that out, Min. All I had to do was pay attention."

She eased her head back, arms still circling his waist. Her gaze met his, her eyes bright and crystal clear. "I feel like I spend my entire day trying to justify my dream to my sisters. They don't understand it. But you do."

Sam pulled her a little closer and kissed her on the forehead. His heart was unfortunately heavy, despite her happy reaction. There was information about BMO he had to share with her today. But for right now, he would enjoy every minute of her gratitude. He rarely felt so rewarded for his efforts.

"Of course I understand it. In fact, I probably get it more than the average person. There are plenty of days when you're leading the charge on everything on your own. I'm in that same boat with my company. The rewards are great when it works out, but it's incredibly stressful when it isn't quite what you want it to be."

"Yes. You are so right. Today feels like one of those days when everything is working out exactly like I want it to."

Sam cringed inwardly, knowing what he had to tell her about Matthew and the way the original sale of the Mercer had happened. But he would let himself savor this beautiful moment for a little longer.

"This corner of the building has an incredible view," Sam said, nodding toward the windows. "Is this where you planned to put your office?"

Mindy trailed over to the corner, glancing outside. "You know, it's funny, but I've envisioned everything else about BMO moving into this space. Except for my office. That part hasn't really registered. Maybe because I've been stuck at Eden's this whole time."

"So you're having a hard time remembering what it used to be like to run BMO." Sam took the checkered blanket he brought and spread it out on the hardwood floor. He took a seat and offered his hand to Mindy.

She settled in right next to him, tucking her legs under her skirt. "Sort of. I mean, I still get to deal with the headaches. Some things are not going well."

Sam had worried that might be the case. He opened the basket and handed Mindy a sandwich from the gourmet shop down the street from his office. He got out a bottle of wine, one that came with a screw cap, and poured some for both of them in small plastic cups. "Cheers."

"To the Mercer," Mindy said.

Sam knew that was his opening. "Min, I need to tell you something about the building. I got the building for a steal. Way under its current value. And I know you said that you were trying to buy it, but I talked to the head of my acquisitions team and he told me that there were no other offers on the property."

Mindy finished chewing a bite of her sandwich, then wiped her mouth with a napkin. "No. That's not right. I signed our offer. I had to as majority owner of the company."

"Do you think it's possible the offer was never actually submitted?"

Mindy reared back her head. "No way. Matthew told me he did it. Why would he lie to me about that? He wanted the building just as badly as I did."

Sam nodded. "I don't know why he would lie, but I'm worried he did."

"What? I can see those gears turning in your head. You're thinking something and I need to know what it is."

"How much do you trust this Matthew guy?"

"He came very highly recommended. Every company he's ever run has been nothing less than supersuccessful. And he's brought a bunch of companies back from the brink of failure."

"That's not what I asked. I asked if you trust him. Do you?"

Mindy sighed and she hunched her shoulders. "Not really."

"I see."

"I figured that was just because it's my company and I'm a control freak and don't really trust anyone when it comes to this."

"Okay, well, here's the other piece of this puzzle that I know about. Our acquisitions team got a tip about the Mercer. We were told to bid quickly and bid low but do an all-cash deal. They checked it out, the building was a great buy and they pulled the trigger. But nobody can tell me exactly where the tip came from."

"None of this makes sense. Why would Matthew want to sabotage the attempt to buy the building? Our only other option was looking at new construction or hoping something better came along. It was a huge setback when we didn't get it."

"Maybe he's trying to sabotage you. Either he's in a competitor's back pocket or, what I think is a more likely scenario, he's seen firsthand that you have a real gem on your hands, but you're in a vulnerable position right now. This is pretty much the time when businesses like yours either fail or flourish. I'm wondering if maybe he's pushing you just close enough to failure to make you want to sell to him."

"People do that?"

"Are you kidding? All the time. Especially guys like Matthew. He runs companies. He doesn't come up with ideas. He has no expertise in building a team. He only knows how to run with existing ones. But you have a pretty amazing setup, you have unlimited growth potential and, most important, he already knows that you're distracted by another big business."

"Eden's."

"Right. You have another year where your attention has to be divided between the two. I'm guessing that he's hoping that you'll give up on one."

"But I would never give up on BMO. It's my baby."

Sam felt a sharp pain in his chest just hearing the distress in Mindy's voice. "I know that. And I'm sure he knows that on some level, too. But he's hoping that at some point, you're going to give your baby up for adoption."

Mindy's jaw was set tight. She seemed confused and stressed out. "Can you help me figure this out? Help me try to decide if this is what's really going on? You're the only one who can do it. If my sisters get involved, he'll know something is up."

"What about me, though? He knows we're exes."

"And maybe that's why he picked you to tip off. He knew it made it a plausible story that you would have swooped in and bought the building."

"We were seen at your sister's wedding together. So it looks like we're back together." Sam didn't say it, but it felt that way, too. It felt like they were a couple, for real. He didn't want to think about what was coming at the end of their week together, when Mindy would once again be under the influence of her family.

Mindy took another bite of her sandwich, and Sam took his chance to eat something, too. Meanwhile, the gears were clearly turning in Mindy's head. He did love seeing her spring to action. "If your hunch is correct, maybe it's a good thing if he thinks we're back together. That should make him plenty nervous, shouldn't it?"

Sam smiled wide. He loved the way she was looking at this. "Yes. And nervous people make mistakes."

"Which means it'll make him even more nervous when he finds out you sold me the building for a dollar." Mindy sipped her wine, then leaned over and kissed him, her sweetness lingering on his lips. "Thank you again, by the way."

"You're so sexy when you're being calculating," he said.

"You're so sexy when you're helping me squash all of my problems. Now we just need to figure out how to squash this one."

Eight

Two days after he sold the Mercer to Mindy, Sam arrived home from work to what was becoming a regular occurrence in his apartment—Mindy, cooking in his kitchen. In heels and a designer dress, no less.

"I see you're at it again," he said, coming up behind her and kissing her neck.

"I had the worst day."

"Most people just have a drink." He reached around to the countertop to a pile of grated parmesan she'd left on the cutting board. "Ooh. Why is cheese so good?"

"I don't know, but I do know that cheese is the

best part of anything with cheese in it." She took a wineglass from the cabinet, poured some for him and topped off her own. "Cheers. Here's to letting the day fall away."

"Cheers." To anyone else, this scene might be nothing but mundane, but to Sam, it was extraordinary. So this was what cohabitation was like. So this was what it was like when Mindy and Sam didn't have anyone between them.

Although Mindy had said she'd had a bad day, she seemed to be in a good mood. Much better than he tended to be when things at work became overwhelming. She buzzed around the room, opening the fridge, adjusting burners and cutting vegetables.

"What happened? Something at Eden's?" he asked.

"Actually, stuff at Eden's is pretty much on autopilot at this point. So much of the staff has been there forever. It's BMO stuff again. Stupid stuff. Totally preventable. The art director not talking to the marketing team. The head of production letting us run out of things a printing business should never run out of." She took another sip of her wine, looked up at the ceiling shaking her head, then pointed her sights at him. "Like paper. Actual paper."

"Seriously?"

"Seriously."

Sam sat down on a bar stool next to the kitchen peninsula. "Do you think it's Matthew?"

Mindy shrugged. "I honestly don't know. I had a call with him today. He claims that he's working on it, and everything he tells me seems to check out, but I just don't know. It feels like somebody is setting little fires everywhere, just so I can run and put them out."

Sam felt a bit like he was about to set a big fire square in the middle of Mindy's work life, and he hated it. But he also knew that the truth would ultimately be so much better for her. "I have some info I want to share with you. I did some digging into Matthew. And I discovered some interesting stuff."

"Good interesting or bad interesting?"

"I don't think you'll be happy. But maybe this is for the best." He unzipped his laptop bag and pulled out a file folder. "Here's what we found."

"We?"

"I'm no detective. I mean, I found some of this on my own, but I also have people who work for me who are exceptionally good at digging." Saying it out loud made him feel bad that he'd taken this step without asking her first.

Mindy wiped her hands on a kitchen towel and joined him at the kitchen peninsula, settling in next to him. "Okay, then. Show me what you found."

Sam opened the folder and walked her through the documents—a mix of online articles about businesses Matthew had run, financial reports and timelines, all of which had a recurring second character—a man named Zeke Anderson. There was a very regular pattern of one of them working their way into a high position within a promising start-up, things going from good to great and then suddenly starting to take a downward turn. At which point the other person, either Matthew or Zeke, swept in and offered to buy a majority stake in the company, just to "rescue" a struggling owner. The companies all miraculously recovered and went on to record earnings.

Mindy clasped her hand over her mouth. "Oh, my God, Sam. This is not only exactly what's happening with BMO, but Matthew suggested to me today that I should consider selling the company before we do the move. So I wouldn't have to deal with the hassle and could just cash in."

"Did you tell him that I sold you the Mercer?"

"I did. He didn't seem fazed by it, but he did bring up the idea of selling right after I told him."

Sam worried that Mindy had a real mess on her hands. He hoped he could figure out a way to help her through it. "I wish I had better news to deliver."

"Me, too. I also wish this had never happened. I feel like a complete idiot for putting my company in jeopardy like this. I clearly didn't do a good enough job vetting this guy."

Sam shook his head emphatically, wanting her to understand that the situation she was in was not of her own doing. "You cannot blame yourself for this.

It's not you, Min. You're a brilliant businesswoman. Look at the companies these two have gotten involved with. Most are hugely successful. That's how they get the next gig and keep themselves looking like geniuses."

"Meanwhile, they're orchestrating the whole thing."

"That's my gut."

"I don't want to let him get to the point where he gets to be the hero. I want to stop him as soon as we can."

"Well, yeah. Of course. If anyone is going to be the hero in this story, it has to be you. I'm here for whatever you need."

Mindy looked at Sam, her eyes bright and full of life. No one could blame her if she were feeling down or defeated by any of this, but she wasn't. She was leaning into the wind, ready to tackle her problems head-on. "Will you help me figure out how to catch him at his own game? At least enough for me to force him out? He has a pretty ironclad contract with us. Unfortunately, I worried more about him not sticking around than I ever worried about needing to get rid of him."

Sam hadn't sorted out how they would do this, but he was fairly certain he could come up with something. "I'm sure I can think of something. Might involve some cloak-and-dagger work. Corporate espionage is no small matter."

Mindy's eyes glinted with mischief. "Ooh. I feel like I'm fully stepping into your dark and sexy underhanded world, Sam."

Sam laughed quietly. "Trust me, it's not that sexy." He cleared his throat when he saw the way Mindy's mouth went slack. That vision of her mouth made him want to take her, right then and there. "Scratch that. With you in it, it's supersexy. Like unbelievably sexy."

Mindy slid off her bar stool and stood between Sam's legs, wagging her hips back and forth, knocking herself against his knees. "You are amazing. Truly amazing. Thank you for showing me the light of day with Matthew. If it wasn't for you, I would be barking up the wrong tree right now, worried about little stuff while much bigger issues were going on under my nose."

"We make a great team." The words had left his lips before he'd really had a chance to think them out.

She smiled and leaned into him. "We make an amazing team."

Once again, Sam was overcome with relief. He'd made so many mistakes in the past and he wanted to prove to her this week that he wasn't that guy. He *was* capable of making her happy. He felt like he'd done that today.

He lowered his head, she raised her chin, and their lips met. Passionate and eager, this kiss felt far more potent than any other. A kiss on steroids, turned on at full blast. Mindy combed her fingers into his hair at the nape, digging in her nails, driving him wild. Her tongue wound in circles with his, the kiss wet and hot. He inched forward on the bar stool and she pressed right against his crotch with her hips, rocking into him as the blood in his veins went from warm to red hot.

He tugged down the zipper of her dress and didn't wait until the garment was off before he was unhooking her bra. Mindy let go of their kiss and shook the straps from her arms, leaving both items of clothing to fall to the floor. He dropped his feet to the floor and picked her up at the waist, plopping her down on the kitchen counter.

She was as tempting as could be sitting before him in nothing more than heels and a pair of lacy black panties. "Much better," he said, taking her breasts in his hands. Her skin was soft as the finest silk, her nipples hard beneath his touch. He drew one tight bud into his mouth, swirling his tongue, savoring her sweetness. How he loved feeling the reaction of her body against his lips, her skin puckering from his touch.

He reached down and curled his fingers into her perfectly round bottom, urging her closer to the edge of the counter. He put one of her legs on his shoulder, then the other, and using his thumb, pulled aside her panties, leaving her bare to him. Mindy planted her hands back behind her, tilting her pelvis and giving him the perfect angle. He lowered his mouth against her center, and licked, slowly at first, listening to her soft moans—pure music to his ears. Making her happy, bringing her close to the brink of orgasm, left everything in his body impossibly tight. It felt as if the blood had left his head and feet and instead raced to his hips, pulsing hard. Mindy bucked her hips, her breaths becoming short and fast.

"Come for me, darling," he said, slipping two fingers inside her. She was so warm, so wet, and he could hardly wait to be inside her, especially as his erection grew harder and heavier between his legs. Still, he wasn't willing to do anything but focus on her pleasure, so he returned to his charge, swirling his tongue in circles while his fingers glided in and out of her body. She gasped loudly when she came, pressing her calves against his back, nearly squeezing his head between her knees. He gave her center one more kiss, which made her suck in a sharp breath.

She lowered her legs and he stood, kissing her deeply. Mindy wrapped her legs around his waist and pulled him closer. "I need more of you," she said. "All of you."

That was exactly what he wanted to give her, but as tall as he was, the cabinet was still in the way. So were his clothes and shoes and far too many other

things. "I don't want to have sex in the kitchen, if
that's okay with you." He didn't wait for a response,
wrapping one arm around her waist and scooping
her legs up in his other arm. Mindy wasn't a damsel
in distress. She didn't need to be saved. But he loved
having the chance to feel for at least a few moments
like he might be her knight in shining armor.

Mindy curled into Sam as he carried her down the
hall to his bedroom, his strides long and confident.
She felt so sexy in his arms, especially in that post-
orgasm glow. The man had the most talented tongue,
the sexiest mouth. And he knew exactly how to send
her over the cliff. When it came to the physical, he
knew exactly how to make her happy.

They arrived in his room and he left the light behind, setting her down on the mattress. She wasn't
about to get settled, though. Sam had taken off his
shirt, and shoes, but his pants had to go. She scram-
bled off the bed and shimmied her panties down her
legs. Then she went to work, getting rid of his pants
and boxer briefs. Sam spent most of his day looking
perfectly yummy to Mindy, but tonight he looked
even better than usual. Maybe it was because she
knew now that he wanted to protect her. No man had
ever wanted to do that, let alone try. She was strong
and independent, but there was still this part of her
inside that was soft and gooey and needed to know
that somebody would be there to catch her fall.

She took Sam's erection in her hand, which immediately produced a deep groan from his lips. She stroked firmly, trying to match the tension beneath his skin with pressure of her own. She felt a little bit like she was losing at this idea, but Sam was more than pleased, his lips humming with approval. She kneeled on the bed and took him into her mouth, skimming her wet lips along his steely length, gripping his hips with her hands. She pressed her thumbs into his skin hard, and that made him growl. She'd learned by now that Sam really liked the contrasts—the hard with the soft, the rough with the tender.

She wrapped her hand around the base of his erection and gently pulled him from her mouth. She rubbed her thumb along the tender underside, enjoying the power she wielded in this situation. She knew she could do anything she wanted and he would be happy. But the reality was that she was most interested right now in what would make them both happy—him inside her. So she eased back on the bed and stretched her arms high above her head, clasping her hands. She was his for the taking and he did exactly that. Descending on her, blazing a hot trail of kisses from her stomach up to her breasts, then settling in her neck just as he drove inside.

The pressure was intense from the very beginning. He filled her so perfectly and they once again fell into that rhythm that made them both happy.

He used one hand to keep her in place, leaving her deliciously defenseless. Meanwhile he slipped his other hand between their bodies, resting his thumb on her center, backed by his complete body weight. Mindy already felt like she was about to rocket into the upper atmosphere, but she told herself to relax, to savor every deft stroke he took inside her.

He had his head turned to one side, breathing hard, pressing one shoulder against hers while bucking his hips.

"Kiss me, Sam," she said. As close as they were right now, she needed more of him. She was desperate for all of him the way a person wants cool water on a hot day.

He claimed her mouth with his, their tongues tangled, and the pressure in her hips coiled so tight she nearly bit Sam's lips. His thrusts were as deep as she could imagine, and she pressed hard on his backside with her feet, raising her hips to meet his. The pleasure was making her light-headed, like she was fading into dark and coming back to light. As good as she knew the climax would be, there was a part of her that wanted this to go on forever. She never wanted to be anywhere else but right there. With Sam.

His hips moved faster and his breaths followed suit. Mindy was on the edge, but she wanted to wait for him. She wanted to get there at the same time. Still, her body was chipping away at her resolve, going tight. Then tighter. And even tighter again. It felt as though fireworks were going off in her body, a chaotic onslaught of electric pulses. Sam froze for a moment and buried his face in her neck, then he took labored thrusts, pulsing inside her over and over again. Mindy didn't dare let go of her legs around him.

When he tried to roll to her side, she followed.

Sam laughed. "It's okay to let go, you know."

"I don't want to," she said, kissing his chest and drinking in his smell. She'd just had two powerful orgasms and she wanted only more of him.

"Well, I'm going to need at least a half hour to recover from that. Maybe more."

Mindy sighed. "Okay. But I just want to stay in bed for the rest of the night, okay?"

"What about the dinner you made?"

"Oh, yeah. I forgot about that. Okay. I just need to pop in some pasta, then we can eat in bed and watch TV and have sex again."

Sam kissed her on the forehead. "Pasta and sex. You really are a dream woman, aren't you?"

He traipsed off to the bathroom and Mindy grabbed one of Sam's T-shirts, then scurried out to the kitchen, turning on the flame under the pot of water she'd left out earlier. The sauce was already prepared. It wouldn't take much more than ten minutes once the water came to a boil.

Sam appeared moments later in his boxers and

poured them each another glass of wine. "I don't think I've ever seen you in just a T-shirt. I'm so used to the designer version of you."

"I can go get my robe if you want. I just grabbed this because it was quicker. I'm highly motivated by the idea of eating in bed."

Sam grinned. "No. I like it. It gives me this idea of what you might have been like when you were younger." He set down his wineglass and formed his fingers into a frame, peering at her through it. "I see seventeen-year-old Mindy Eden, making spaghetti in the kitchen of the family mansion."

"I wouldn't call it a mansion. It was a penthouse." Mindy always got a little defensive when the privilege of her youth was brought up. Yes, she'd had anything material she could have ever wanted, but there hadn't been a lot of love and affection in that household, aside from what was between Sophie and Mindy. It was a big part of the reason they were so close.

"What were you like as a teenager?" he asked.

"Pretty much the way I am now. I've always been focused on accomplishing things. Staying busy. Keeping myself occupied. Otherwise, I get bored."

"So you weren't running around with your friends chasing after guys?"

Mindy gave the pasta sauce a stir. "Oh, no. I did my fair share of that."

"Lots of boyfriends?"

"Lots of dates. Not many who stuck around very long. I had a tendency to pick guys who thought like my dad. Guys who didn't like the fact that I was driven. They wanted a girl who would sit back and let them be at center stage. I'm just not like that. I don't have to be the center of attention, but I'm not going to set aside my dreams for a guy."

"How could your dad not admire that in a daughter?"

"He had a lot of preconceived ideas about what a girl should be like. I also think he wished I'd been a boy. I was the firstborn. I wasn't much of an heir in his mind." Mindy fought back the sad feelings that came along with this topic. She had enough confused thoughts and guilt about her dad to last a lifetime. She'd never felt loved by him. Not once. Still, she wanted to share this part of herself with Sam. Maybe it would help him see that she wasn't as indestructible as he thought.

"I guess you eventually got past the stage of picking guys like your dad?"

"Not really. Honestly, you're the first one who wasn't entirely like him. Of course, it was a little different with you. You pursued me. I'm not sure I would have had the guts to approach you the night we met."

Sam reared back his head. "You don't strike me as a woman who has any problem introducing herself to a man."

She smiled and lifted the top off the pot of water, dumping in half a box of bucatini pasta. She gave it a healthy dose of salt, a stir, and set the timer for nine minutes. "You're a little too intimidating, Sam."

"Physically, maybe. But I'm not once you get to know me."

She shook her head. "No. You can still be intimidating. You play things very close to the vest. You get closed off sometimes. In that way, you're a lot like my dad."

"I don't mean to be that way. It's just my personality."

He turned away from her, walking across the kitchen, getting a water glass from the cabinet and filling it at the fridge. It was a perfectly innocent act—he was thirsty. But she couldn't help but feel like he was doing the exact thing she'd just brought up. He was closing himself off, when all she wanted was to talk. He'd mentioned in passing at Sophie's wedding that his mom had passed away when he was a teen. She wondered if he'd open up to her about it.

"What about you? What were you like as a teenager?" she asked.

He drew a deep breath through his nose, then downed the rest of his water. "Sullen. Moody."

Mindy didn't want to immediately jump to the conclusion that he was that way because of his mother. Surely there had been some happy times. "What about girls?"

"Not until college."

"Really?"

"Really."

Mindy was getting the distinct impression that he did not want to talk about this. She didn't want to push. Not when they were having such a perfect night. She wasn't going to ruin it with questions and prying. If Sam wanted to open up to her, he would. She only hoped it would happen eventualiy. She needed to be close to him. In more ways than one.

Nine

By Sunday night, Mindy was cooking again. She couldn't help it. It was the only way she could cope with her anxiety, and it was much healthier than downing entire bottles of wine. Sam had gone for a run, which left Mindy to do nothing but think about the week ahead. Being pulled in so many directions was making her feel like she was losing her mind. She couldn't handle the constant push and pull—she was stuck between Eden's and BMO, stuck between wanting to believe Matthew and not trusting him at all, and most difficult of all was the spot she was in between her sisters and Sam. Sophie and Emma would both be back at Eden's tomorrow, which meant that a storm was moving in.

She and Sam had given themselves a week. Tomorrow morning was supposed to be the end. Logic said that she should move her things out, that these seven days had been nothing but a fantasy fulfilled. But that thinking was too focused on logic and right now she was feeling more like she wanted to follow her heart. She didn't want to leave. She wanted to stay put. But was that her wanting to hide from her problems? It wasn't like she and Sam were ready to move in together. Not for real. Plus, she knew exactly what Sophie and Emma would say if they knew where she was right now. Forget the bet—even if that had never existed, they would be shaking her out of her dream state, reminding her that she had deluded herself many times when it came to Sam. She and Sam had enjoyed stretches of happiness before and it always went south. Always.

Sam's home phone rang, and Mindy jumped at the sound. Sam always got calls on his cell. She hadn't heard this line ring once while she'd been here. She shuffled to the far side of the kitchen counter and squinted at the caller ID, but it displayed Private Number, so she let it go to voice mail. Back at the stove, tending some sautéed mushrooms, the phone stopped ringing, but only for a few seconds before it started up again. Once more, Private Number. Whoever was calling certainly wanted to get through. Maybe there was some sort of emergency. Maybe it was Sam and his cell was acting up again.

"Hello?" she answered, cradling the receiver between her ear and shoulder while carefully trimming the ends of green beans.

"Uh, hi. I'm looking for Sam. Who's this?"

It was a woman's voice, one Mindy did not recognize. "Who's this?"

"Sam's sister. Isabel."

Sister? Sam had never, ever mentioned that he had a sister. Not even the other night when she'd tried to ask what he was like as a teenager. What the hell was going on?

"I don't want to be a jerk, but again, I'd like to ask who's answering my brother's phone," Isabel said. "And is he there? I need to speak to him."

Mindy stopped working and set the knife on the marble counter. "Sorry. I was in the middle of making dinner and got distracted. This is Mindy. Mindy Eden." For a moment, she considered whether or not she should label herself—girlfriend? Houseguest?

"Oh, my God. You're the one who broke my brother's heart."

"Excuse me?" This was all too much to process at one time. A sister? And Mindy as the heartbreaker? More like the other way around. It was officially time to pour herself a glass of wine. Sam might have kept his sister hidden from her, but he'd apparently had no problem telling his sister about her.

"He told me all about you," Isabel said. "I know every last thing about you and your crazy family."

Mindy didn't even know what to say. Part of her wanted to defend herself, part of her knew that it was the truth—she loved her family, but crazy things did tend to be part and parcel of being an Eden. "Sam's not here right now. He went for a run. Would you like me to tell him that you called?"

Isabel laughed quietly. "You're changing the subject. I'm sorry. I shouldn't have said that. I'm just very protective of Sam. I don't like to see him get hurt."

"Understandable. I'm the same way about my sisters." Mindy turned off the burner on the stove and took a seat at the kitchen peninsula. "I don't know how to say this, but he never told me about you. He never mentioned anyone but his mom. And that was only in passing."

"Interesting."

"What? Tell me why that's interesting." Mindy realized how desperate she was for information. It was like a portal into Sam had opened up before her and she wanted to peer inside before it closed. "Please."

"If he didn't tell you about me, it only means that he doesn't trust you. Not completely, anyway. Sam's secretive, but most of that comes from things that happened when we were kids. He had to grow up very fast. And I couldn't always be there to help."

None of this was answering anything. It was only leaving Mindy with more questions. It was also saddling her with a growing sadness, one so big it was threatening to swallow her whole. Sam didn't trust her. That wasn't a guess. She had hard evidence of it. "Can you tell me more?"

"If you know about the fundraiser he's hosting, that explains a lot of it."

"No. I don't know anything about it." Now her sadness was becoming outright despair. She'd really fooled herself, hadn't she? She'd thought she and Sam were getting closer this week. Now she knew she was wrong.

"Well, you might want to ask him about that. Or not. I don't know the state of your relationship, but considering the fact that you're answering his home phone, I'd guess you two are back together."

"It's complicated." Mindy hardly knew Isabel. She wasn't going to offer more.

"I'm guessing he would say the same thing."

"Probably."

"Well, let him know that I called, please. I tried his cell but I couldn't get through."

"I will." Mindy said goodbye and returned the phone to its cradle, but was left with a more unsettled feeling than she'd had before she answered the call. She'd been looking forward to a nice night with Sam. Clearly there were things that needed to be discussed.

From the other side of the apartment, Mindy heard Sam's front door close. "Hello?" Sam called out, appearing in the kitchen moments later, sweaty from his run and with a wide grin across his face. Mindy simply watched him as he closed in on her, the unease from the phone call abating for the moment, replaced by the thrill of being in the same space with him.

Sam surveyed the landscape of the countertops and island, where Mindy's cooking project was strewn about. "Hi. I'm looking for Mindy Eden. She's tall. Gorgeous. Real ball of fire. The last time I saw her was a little less than two hours ago and she had not yet turned my kitchen into a war zone."

She stepped closer to him, feeling even more conflicted than she had when she'd come home to start dinner. She was over the moon to see him, but there were uncomfortable subjects ahead. Big decisions to be made. "You're funny. So funny." She didn't care that he was sweaty. She just wanted to be close to him. She wrapped her arms around him, pressing herself against the hard plane of his chest. It was hard to escape the feeling that this was where she belonged, but was that just wishful thinking? Was she pinning hope on a situation that wasn't real? That didn't really exist? Isabel's phone call right before Sam walked in the door certainly felt like a sign. It was without question a reminder—Sam had secrets. She knew it.

The kitchen timer buzzed, pulling them out of their quiet moment. "That's the gratin. Time to take it out of the oven." She hustled over to the stove.

"Smells amazing."

Mindy placed the ceramic casserole dish on the stove, wanting to get past the mental block that was stuck in her head. "Before I forget, you got a phone call."

"You answered my phone?"

"Well, yeah. I've never heard it ring before. It startled me. And I guess I thought it might be important. Your cell phone is always acting up."

"Next time, you can feel free to let it go to voice mail."

Now this was officially not sitting well with Mindy. "It was your sister. Isabel? The sister I had no idea you had."

Sam craned his neck, looking up at the ceiling, drawing a breath through his nose. "I really wish you hadn't answered the phone."

"Do you want to tell me about her? Or would you rather keep expressing the idea that I have somehow crossed the line by daring to answer your phone?"

"Well, you did cross the line. I would never do that at your place."

"So you trust me to sleep in your bed or make

dinner in your kitchen, but you don't trust me to take a message? You trust me with a key to your apartment, but you don't trust me with this?" Mindy was more than hurt. She'd thought she and Sam had been making progress. Moving forward. Now it all felt like a lie. "I'm sorry, but that's insulting, and I can't help but be hurt. You have a sister and you never told me about her."

"Min, I really don't think you should be lecturing me about trust. It's more than a little hypocritical considering that there have been many times when as soon as something goes wrong, you look to me."

Sam was right. He was absolutely right. "I'm sorry. I don't know what I'm doing anymore. I shouldn't have answered your phone. Especially when we both know that what's between us has been temporary."

"Oh, right. Tomorrow is the day you surrender to your sisters."

"Don't you understand? I'm not giving in to my sisters. I'm not letting them determine my future, just because they think they know what's right for me. I'm not letting them keep me from everything I've worked so hard for, but I need to be able to do it on my own terms. No guilt."

"You realize a future is about more than what you do for work all day."

Mindy just looked at him, his words tumbling

around in her head and getting stuck in a perpetual loop. "You live for your work."

"I do, but after this week, I'm starting to see that maybe I want more."

More of what? Her? Was that possible? If so, that meant that he needed to stop hiding things from her. "If you're suggesting you want more with me, I don't see how we're going to make that work if you're getting upset with me for answering the phone. And especially not when you're keeping family members a secret, especially ones who know about me. Who know about us."

"Oh, no. Did Isabel say something?"

"She referred to me as the woman who broke your heart."

"She doesn't have much of a filter. I'm sorry."

"Is that true, Sam? Did you talk to her about me? Did you say that? And I don't understand why you wouldn't tell me about her. I don't think you realize how much it hurts to have you shut me out like that."

Sam then did the same thing he did the other night—he turned away from her. Except this time, he walked right out of the room, over to the bank of tall windows in the living room. A person could accuse Sam Blackwell of many things, but he did not shy away from confrontation. You could call him out on the most horrible thing in the world and he would own up to it if the deed was his own. This secretiveness was making Mindy sick to her stomach. This was all wrong. "Sam? Are you going to talk to me?"

He shook his head, not looking at her.

"Are you serious?" She stepped closer and attempted to look him in the eye, but he avoided her. And he did not say a thing.

Mindy couldn't stay. She couldn't endure this. Not the quiet. This was the sort of thing her dad always did when he was angry—he'd kill everyone with silence. It was the cruelest form of punishment to have someone refuse to engage. "If you aren't going to talk to me, I can't stay."

Sam didn't move. Not a single twitch of a muscle. He just stood there in the dim light of the living room, staring off through the windows at the city.

"Okay, then," she said, her voice shaking. She turned on her heel and walked out of the room, past the kitchen and away from the meal she'd prepared. It would just have to go cold. Sam would have to clean up the mess himself. She had to get out of this apartment. Sure enough, the end had come for them. She'd thought it would be tomorrow. But what was the difference? In the end, this thing with Sam was made of glimpses of happiness strung between everything else that was wrong.

She stalked into his bedroom, flipped on the light and grabbed one of her garment bags, spreading it out on the bed. She took her clothes from the closet in handfuls, tossing them in haphazardly and not caring that she was going too fast and rumpling everything. If she did this quickly enough, she and Sam wouldn't have to speak another word to each other. That was clearly what he wanted. With her clothes gathered, she went into the bathroom, scooping up makeup and dumping it into her cosmetic bag. She avoided her own reflection in the mirror. It would be hard enough to live in her own brain tonight. She wasn't going to give herself a visual reminder of how much she hated some of the circumstances of being Mindy Eden.

Sam appeared at the bathroom door. "Don't go. Please don't go."

Mindy clamped her eyes shut, wishing she could ward off the effect of his voice. "I refuse to stay if you won't talk to me. I won't do it."

He stepped closer and she dared to look up into his dark eyes. "Let me tell you about Isabel. Let me tell you about everything."

The absolute last thing Sam ever wanted to be was vulnerable. Life was easier when you played everything close to the vest. He never let anyone see his soft spots. It not only made his weaknesses easier to ignore, it made it that much more difficult for anyone to hurt him. He'd been knocked down plenty in his first eighteen or so years. He wasn't going to intentionally invite it on himself.

But that was before Mindy started packing her things and preparing to walk out of his life.

"I'm serious," he said. "Don't go."

Mindy took the armful of makeup she had and set it all back down on the bathroom countertop. "I can't deal with the silent treatment. My dad used to do that to Sophie and my mom and me and it's the absolute worst."

"I know it's bad."

"I tried to be respectful the other night when you didn't want to talk about what you were like as a teenager, but I can't deal with secrets, either. I'm not expecting you to tell me everything, but I at least expect there to be some attempt at showing me the boundaries. Half of the time I feel like I'm stumbling around in the dark with you."

Funny, but Sam felt the exact same way about Mindy. And not just half of the time. All the time. "What do you want to know?"

"For starters, I want to know about Isabel. I want to know why you didn't tell me about her. I also want to know about this fundraiser you're hosting. You haven't said a peep about that to me."

Wow, Isabel had really gotten her mouth running. "She jumped the gun if she told you about that. I haven't committed to the fundraiser. And it's all intertwined. It's all connected."

"Okay, then. Just tell me. You can trust me, Sam. I promise."

Sam took Mindy's hand. "Am I going to ruin dinner if I tell you about Isabel? And my mom? It's not a short story."

"I couldn't care any less about dinner right now, Sam. If you want to share even the tiniest bit of yourself with me, I'll take it."

Had Sam left Mindy feeling like she was scrounging for crumbs? That had never been his intention. "Okay. Let's sit." He led her over to the bed, where they both settled in on the edge. He wasn't sure where to start—he had never, ever told anyone about his mom, except for the woman at the ALS Foundation, and that was still only the broadest of strokes. He hadn't told her about losing his dad as a direct result of his mother's illness. He hadn't told her how his entire family, the only family he'd ever known, completely fell apart.

"Isabel is three years older than me. We were always close, but we became more so when our mom was diagnosed with ALS."

"Lou Gehrig's disease?"

"Yes. Exactly. I was fourteen. Isabel was just finishing high school. Our mom was young. Only thirty-nine. She'd been losing strength in her hands and had a hard time holding on to even the simplest of things, like the handle on a coffeepot. When her voice started to change, a neighbor suggested she see a doctor." Just getting that much of his story out felt like a huge accomplishment, especially as visions of his past shuttled through his mind—the morning his mom dropped the coffee carafe on the kitchen floor and it shattered. The day their parents gathered his sister and him in the living room to deliver the terrible news, trying to frame it as something they would all get through. And, ultimately, the sacrifice their father decided to make to save his children's future.

"Sam, I am so sorry. You mentioned at the wedding that she passed away when you were still a teenager."

"She lived a little more than three years after that. So I was seventeen. It was halfway through my senior year of high school. It was not easy, especially since I was the only one around to care for her at that point. Isabel was away at college."

"What about your dad? Was he not a part of your life? You don't talk about him, either."

This was the cruel twist of fate in Sam's life story. In a way, his mother's disease claimed his father, too. "He died in a car accident almost a year before our mom passed. Went right into a guardrail on his way to work. But it wasn't an accident. He took his own life. I know this because he left me a note and told me he was doing it for the life insurance money. He did it for Isabel and me." Sam heard his own voice crack, and he wasn't sure which was worse—the actual sound or the way Mindy's expression morphed into profound sadness. "The medical bills had piled up and I'd gotten early acceptance to Stanford. Isabel was already at Columbia and had applied for law school. He told me to take care of my mom, pay off the house and the bills, and to get myself to Stanford. He also told me to burn the note. So that's what I did."

Sam cast his sights up to the ceiling, fighting back the tears that were welling in his eyes. He hadn't truly broken down since the day his mom passed away. He'd told himself that he couldn't afford to show emotion. He'd never felt weaker than on that day, not even on the day when his dad had died. That day had been more about shock than anything.

Mindy scooted closer and pulled him into her arms, cradling the back of his head with her hand and letting him rest his cheek on her shoulder. She held him so tight it felt like she might squeeze the life out of him, and maybe that was for the best—the only times he'd truly felt alive in recent history were when he was with her. And she was going to leave tomorrow and there was nothing to be done about that. She'd never been anything less than crystal clear about her priorities—family first, job and career a close second and Sam a distant third. Not that he could blame her for her choices. Except for selling the Mercer to her for a dollar, he'd done nothing but put his own business front and center. But he had his reasons. Money bought security. It bought permanence in a world where everything is fleeting. He wouldn't apologize for needing that.

"I wish I knew what to say." Mindy sniffled and he felt the dampness of her tears on his nose when he raised his head and kissed her cheek. "I had no idea. That's the saddest story I think I have ever heard."

"I don't want you to feel sorry for me, Min. I really don't. It was a long time ago and everyone has a sad story, don't they? I'm no different than anyone else."

"But you keep it all bottled up inside. It's not good for you. And the only support system you have is your sister, and you hid her, too."

"Are you trying to make me feel better? Because it isn't working."

Mindy cracked a small smile and laughed quietly. "Sorry. My bedside manner isn't the best." She took one of his hands and pulled it into her lap. With her other hand, she combed her fingers through his hair.

It was such a sweet and tender gesture, it made Sam want to say that he never ever wanted Mindy to leave. But he knew for a fact that if he were going to scare Mindy, that was the way to do it. She didn't want to be tied down. Her own mother had told him as much. "So now you know why I clammed up the other night. As for the fundraiser, they've asked me to host, stepping in for the original sponsor.

I've always been a big donor, but I don't want to be the public face of the event. I just don't think I can do that. I told them I'd give them the money, but I'm not sure about the rest of it. I'd have to make a speech and really put myself out there. You know it's more my inclination to hide in the shadows."

"But you've attended the fundraiser before? Listened to other people give those speeches?"

"Yes. And they're gut-wrenching sometimes. So sad."

Mindy nodded patiently and Sam suspected he knew where she was headed with this. "But does it make you feel less alone when you hear other people tell their stories?"

"Well, yeah. I guess."

"So maybe it's your turn, Sam. If you shared your story, it would be another way of giving back. It might help other people deal with their own circumstances or at least come to terms with a loss like the one you experienced."

"That was exactly the pitch the foundation made to me. But I just don't know if I can get up on that stage and talk about all of that."

"If you can tell me, you can tell anybody."

He wanted to tell her that she was the exception in all of this. She was the one he could trust. "That's my point. We know each other and it was still hard. Plus, I'd have to write the speech and it's only a few days away. That's not my area of expertise at all."

"Then let me help you. You can practice on me. I made a great speech at Sophie's wedding. The truth is that you and I make a great team and I think you should let me help you."

Sam wasn't sure what this meant for their relationship, but right now, he wasn't willing to push for anything more than time with her. "What about your sisters? What about the bet? We're going to end up spending time together if we do this."

"As far as I'm concerned, I'm helping a friend. Nothing else."

"So you really think I should do it?"

"I think it could help you heal. And that's important. So yes, I think you should do it."

"Okay, then. I'll call the foundation first thing tomorrow."

Mindy looked at him, scanning his face with her beautiful eyes. "The only other thing we haven't talked about is that bit about me breaking your heart. Does your sister hate me?"

"If she does, at least you know how I feel. Sophie and Emma hate me. I know that."

"I don't know that *hate* is the right word. And maybe the fundraiser will help to change that. I can tell them about it and get them to buy tickets."

Oh, no. It was bad enough to have one member of the Eden family feeling sorry for him. "Don't do that. Please, don't. That'll just make me more nervous anyway."

"Okay. Okay. I won't say a thing." She stared down at her own hands for a moment. "You didn't really feel like I broke your heart, did you? Not really, right?"

Sam had spent more than enough time this evening tearing open his soul and letting Mindy see it all. He didn't think he could take any more. This was a talk for another day. Another time. If she wanted to have the conversation. "*Heartbroken* is such a melodramatic word. *Disappointed* might be more accurate."

Mindy nodded slowly, taking it all in. "Okay. That makes me feel better. I would never want to do that."

Sam would cling to that much from this moment forward. Even if it ended up happening, he would at least know she hadn't wanted to do it. "Are you still going to leave tonight? Or can I at least convince you to stay until morning?"

Mindy pulled her legs up onto the bed and curled into his chest. "For right now, I'm not going anywhere."

Ten

The morning after Sam's big confession, Mindy got up early and reluctantly moved her things out of his apartment. Their week together had not been what she'd expected. She'd thought this might be their last gasp, or at least an escape from her everyday life. To her great surprise, they'd grown closer. She'd seen sides of Sam she'd never known.

But she was hesitant to push for more with Sam. Was one week enough to change everything? She couldn't imagine a scenario in which it would be enough to convince Sophie and Emma to change their minds about him. And if Sam couldn't be folded into her family life, he couldn't be a real part of her love life. No matter the problems with her sisters, they were the two people she could always count on. They stood by her. More than anything, they loved her.

Love was looming large in Mindy's mind. Was that what she was feeling with Sam? She wanted to think so, but was a week enough time to fall in love? There was also the question of how he felt about her. He'd expressed affection in a million unspoken ways, but the words had not passed his lips. There had been no *I love you*, and as brave as Mindy could be, she couldn't be the first to put that out there. Not as the person who'd long questioned whether she was lovable at all.

Standing on the sidewalk outside Sam's apartment, this game of goodbye was a sad one, one in which she was afraid to bring up anything about their relationship. It was easier to talk about the excuses they had to see each other. "You'll call the foundation today? Tell them you'll make a speech at the fundraiser?" she asked.

"As long as you'll be my date. Isabel is going to be there, but I've spent so many years leaning on her. It's difficult for her, too. I need to know that you will be there for me." He had his sunglasses on again, hiding behind them, leaving her with only his words.

"I'll be there. And don't forget your speech," Mindy said, a transparent attempt at stealing a few more precious seconds. "I promised I would help you with that."

"At least let me practice on you. Maybe tomorrow night?"

There was the glimmer she needed—the promise of time with him. Something to look forward to. "Yes. That sounds perfect."

Fighting sadness, Mindy kissed him, but she made it quick. She didn't want a tear to roll down her cheek and cross her lips. She didn't want him to know just how melancholy she was about leaving. With her driver waiting at the curb, this wasn't the time for an extended goodbye anyway. And maybe that was for the best.

Clay rushed Mindy off to Eden's, and she spent the entire car ride fretting over how to handle the Sophie and Emma situation. She was in deeper with Sam. There would be no denying that. Mindy's trust issues with him were fading away. But what would it take for Sophie and Emma to trust that Sam might be good for her? Under the burden of the silly bet, it would be next to impossible. They would use any excuse to keep Mindy at Eden's. Mindy had to convince them to drop the whole thing. Sophie would be the hardest nut to crack.

About an hour after Mindy arrived at the office, Sophie trailed in, so radiant and relaxed it was like she walked on air. "Knock, knock. I'm back." She plopped down on the chair and grinned from ear to ear at Mindy.

"I take it you had a good time?"

"The best. The absolute best. The villa we rented was unbelievable. Right on the water. Private pool. We had the most amazing chef, who cooked for us morning, noon and night. We snorkeled. We spent hours on the beach every morning, then a nap in the afternoon, and that, of course, led to—"

"I don't need to hear every last detail." Mindy not only didn't want to hear about what came after nap time, she couldn't help but be a bit annoyed. She may have had an incredible week with Sam, but it was all in hiding. No matter how good things were, it hadn't been out in the open. They weren't free.

"Are you jealous?" Sophie grimaced. "We were on our honeymoon. I don't know what else you expect me to talk about."

"No. I just don't need to know the blow-by-blow. Literally." Of course, she was at least a little bit envious. She was only human, and she wanted the things that Sophie had in her life—love and commitment.

Emma poked her head into Mindy's office. "Are you guys meeting without me?"

"I just got here." Sophie hopped up out of her seat and Mindy walked out from behind her desk, so the three of them could embrace. "Bali was amazing, but I'm happy to be home. I'm happy we're all back together."

"How was England?" Mindy asked Emma while returning to her place behind her desk.

Emma perched on the empty chair and Sophie sat again. "Well, let's just say I spent a fair amount of time feeling sick." Emma's eyes darted back and forth between Mindy and Sophie.

Oh, my God.

"Wait a second," Sophie blurted. "Are you?"

Emma nodded. "I'm pregnant."

Sophie squealed. Mindy was excited, but that feeling of being left behind also managed to crop up somewhere in the middle of her reaction. Once again, her sisters had their personal lives on track while she was making only small strides in figuring hers out.

"I took a test while we were there," Emma said. "I thought about texting you guys the news, but I didn't want to interrupt the honeymoon, and Mindy's always working, anyway. I thought I would wait until I could tell you both in person."

"When are you due?" Mindy asked.

Emma shook her head. "I don't know, exactly. I just made a doctor's appointment. This wasn't planned at all, but we did have a condom malfunction and that was all it took, apparently."

"What does Daniel think about all of this?" Sophie asked.

"He's so thrilled. He already bought a stuffed animal for the baby. A little bulldog that looks just like Jolly." Emma's cheeks blushed bright pink. "And his mom is warming to me now. A baby changes everything."

"Such amazing news," Mindy said. She meant it, but damn... It was hard to keep a stiff upper lip right now.

"It really is. Congratulations to you both." Sophie crossed her legs and bobbed her foot up and down. "So get us up to speed, Min. What happened during the week?"

"Everything was smooth sailing. Not a single problem." That was a lie, of course, but Mindy had handled the few problems that had cropped up. The one thing Mindy did not need to do was to convince her sisters of her capabilities. "The store practically runs itself."

Sophie narrowed her eyes. "Are you sure? Absolutely nothing bad happened? How did the big cosmetics sale go? I haven't seen the numbers."

"Sales were up seven percent over last year. So definitely a move in the right direction."

"Well, great. That's good." Sophie shrugged and looked over at Emma. "I guess we just get back to work as usual."

"I want to hear about your week, Mindy," Emma said. "Not everything is about us."

Mindy did appreciate Emma's generosity. Sophie

was the one who often put on the blinders. Mindy could have easily launched into a talk about what was going on at BMO, but she didn't want to ignore the one good thing in her life—Sam. It wasn't right that she couldn't talk about it. It wasn't right that she felt like she had to hide.

"I spent the entire week with Sam. I stayed at his apartment, and it was amazing."

"Oh, my God." Sophie sat back in her seat, shaking her head. "So you're giving up? You're ready to lose the bet and have your heart broken? Because you know that's what's going to happen, right? It's always the same thing with him."

Mindy had to stand up for herself. And she had to stand up for the only chance she had right now for personal happiness. "I'm not losing the bet. It's silly, Sophie, and you know it."

"I know nothing of the sort. It's meant to keep you from making a bad choice."

"Sam and I really had an incredible week together. He's not the way you think he is, Soph. I don't care what Jake says."

"It's not just Jake who's coloring my opinion of Sam. It's lots of people. Including you, at times."

"He has made some poor choices," Emma said. "Do you really want to give him another chance? Is he worth it?"

When Emma put it like that, Mindy had to defend him. "He deserves another chance. I believe that. You know, he sold me the Mercer Building for BMO. He sold it to me for a dollar."

"Wait. What? Sam's involved with the deal on the Mercer?"

Mindy had purposely not told Sophie about this before, just so she wouldn't have any reason to question why Sam was her date at the wedding. But now she had no choice but to reveal what was going on behind the scenes. "Yes. It turns out that Sam bought the building before we had a chance to. It was a mix-up on Matthew's part, but it all got worked out. I asked Sam about it and he agreed to sell it to me for BMO."

"Did you know all of this before the wedding? Is that why you brought him? Did you seriously trade him an invitation to my wedding for the right to buy the building?"

"Technically, yes, but he also solved my Gerald problem. And you should be glad he was there anyway. He kept Mom and Emma's mom from killing each other at your reception."

"I don't know that my mom would have actually resorted to that," Emma said. "She's mostly harmless."

"Regardless, Sam does not earn a free pass for calming down a woman at my wedding. And I have to question his motives for selling you the building for a dollar. Who does that?"

"Maybe he's in love with you," Emma said.

"Is he?" Sophie asked. "Did he say that he loves you?"

At first, Mindy experienced a tiny blip of hope. Was giving her the building Sam's way of saying he truly and deeply cared for her? It would be amazing if that were the case, but it felt foolish to hope for such a thing. If Sam wanted to say something, he came out with it. She could only imagine that if he was thinking about something as serious as love, he would have said it. The only secrets he kept were the painful ones. Love wasn't painful. Or at least it wasn't supposed to be. "No. He didn't."

"So again, I'm left with the question of his motives," Sophie said.

Mindy had a deep need to prove to her sister that Sam really was a good guy. "Look. I'm telling you that he's got a big heart. He's hosting a charity fundraiser for ALS research in a few days. He's one of their biggest donors, but this year, he's going to give a talk about losing his mom to the disease. I'm going with him as moral support."

Sophie looked at Mindy with such pity that Mindy felt sick to her stomach. "So he's going for sympathy now? Is that why he has you wrapped around his finger, again?"

Mindy's queasiness had turned into a feeling of hurtling toward earth headfirst. Everything she said got turned back on her. "Why are you being so mean about this, Soph? Is this about winning the bet?"

"Would I love to declare the bet a done deal? Absolutely. But it's not about winning. I'm tired of not knowing that you're going to stay at Eden's for the long haul. Emma and I want you here by our side. We love you, and frankly, we're worried about what you're doing to yourself."

"We know you feel pulled in several different directions," Emma said "We understand that's hard. But maybe if you made a decision on the business side of your life, the personal part might fall into place. You might meet the perfect guy."

Mindy wasn't foolish enough to tell her sisters that she was starting to feel like she had met the perfect guy. It was easier to focus on the business part of this discussion. "But it's not a decision, is it? It's not a choice I get to make," Mindy asked, hating the way her voice was starting to crack. "My inheritance is tied to these two years at Eden's. I can't walk away from that."

"Is it just the money?" Sophie asked. "I'd like to think that you want to be here because of us."

Mindy closed her eyes for a moment. Of course it was about more than that, and it was far more complicated. "I do want to be here because of you two. I actually really enjoy my job at the store. I like feeling like I can fix things. I sure as hell can't fix things at BMO right now."

"I thought things were going great," Sophie said.

Mindy shook her head. "They're not. They're falling apart. And the worst of it is that I think the person who might be making it fall apart is Matthew Hawkins, the man I hired to keep the operation afloat. And I think he's doing it on purpose."

"Why do you think that?" Emma asked.

Mindy told her sisters everything—every last embarrassing detail, including the fact that it had been Sam who figured it out. "So I have to figure out if Matthew really is trying to poach my company."

"How will you do that?" Emma got up and pulled three bottles of water from the small fridge in Mindy's office, handing one each to Mindy and Sophie, then taking a drink of her own.

"I don't know, exactly," Mindy answered. "Do you guys have any ideas?"

Sophie twisted her lips into a tight bundle, clearly putting on her thinking cap. "You could offer to sell him the company. See how he responds. That's what he wants, isn't it?"

"That sounds risky," Mindy said. "He'll want it in writing and then I'll be stuck. I'm not giving that guy any leverage over me at all."

"Do you have an employee you trust?" Emma asked. "Someone who's been there from the beginning and knows the ins and outs of the business?

Maybe they can shed some light on what's going on. Or help you figure it out."

It was typically Mindy's last resort to trust anyone. It was easier to rely only on herself. But this situation called for extreme measures. "Carla Meadows. She was my third employee. She oversees the production. In fact, she's the person Matthew has blamed a lot of our problems on. He's been dealing with her."

"Talk to her," Sophie said. "And most importantly, tell him that you're talking with her. Make him nervous. That's when people start making mistakes."

"That's exactly what Sam says."

"I don't make a habit of agreeing with Sam, but I might have to on this one." Sophie leaned forward, placing both elbows on her knees. "Frankly, I'm surprised he didn't come up with a plan to help you catch Matthew. That seems like his wheelhouse."

"You know, all of that is way more about Sam knowing how to get what he wants, rather than him being particularly underhanded. I have to admire that in him."

"Yeah, well, Jake doesn't."

All Mindy could think was that this would all be solved if Sophie, Jake and Emma were able to see Sam in a different light. She wanted them to see the Sam that she adored. The man she was falling for, even when that was the scariest thing to admit.

"I want you all to come to the fundraiser. I'll buy the tickets."

"Seriously?" Sophie asked, seeming incredulous.

"Yes. It's for an amazing cause and I think it will be good for you to see what he's really like. He's going to give a speech and I think it'll all do us some good." She knew this was a huge gamble. It could very easily backfire.

Lizzie appeared at the door. "I don't want to interrupt, but we just got this letter from a lawyer's office. I had to sign for it. It looks important."

Sophie reached out for the envelope. "I'll take it."

Mindy sat back in her chair, her previous hurt morphing into panic. She was going to have to find a way to break it to Sam that she had not kept the fundraiser a secret. In fact, she'd gone so far as to invite her family to the event. He was going to be horrified. And quite possibly furious.

"Oh, my God," Sophie said, her skin going starkly pale. "A man named Benjamin Summers claims to have a promissory note against Eden's. Not just the building. The land, too. It belonged to his father and it's his now." Sophie stood and placed the letter on Mindy's desk. Emma got up out of her seat and read over Mindy's shoulder.

Unfortunately, one line into the letter Mindy realized she'd made a mistake when she didn't speak to the man who called the day she was going to the Mercer.

"Gram took out a private loan? Why would she do that?" Emma asked.

"I have no idea," Sophie said. "We have to bring in our lawyers right away to look at this. The tone of the letter is so aggressive. And I need to talk to Lizzie. It says that they tried to reach us by phone but were unable to get through."

Mindy raised her hand. "That was me. My fault. I thought it sounded like a scam, so I told Lizzie to just get the guy off the phone. I had no idea it was real."

Sophie blew out an exasperated breath. "Well, now we've apparently made Benjamin Summers very angry. We're going to have to figure this out. Right away."

Mindy was desperate to redeem herself in the eyes of her sisters, not only because of this gaffe, but because she wanted to find a way forward with Sam. She'd never be able to forge a lasting relationship with him if her sisters weren't on board. "Let me handle it. I need to talk to the legal team about some other things, anyway."

"Are you sure?" Sophie asked. "You're the one who's already stretched way too thin."

Mindy shrugged. "I work best under pressure."

"So you really want us to come to this fundraiser? It's going to take some doing to convince Jake," Sophie said.

"Just tell him that if he comes that night and still

hates Sam by the time it's all said and done, then I'll drop the whole thing."

"You mean you'll drop Sam?" Emma asked.

Mindy wasn't willing to go there. Not yet. "I'm not saying that at all. Frankly, I've had enough of wagers and bets."

Eleven

Within twenty-four hours, the situation with Benjamin Summers grew even more complicated and inexplicable. This mysterious man claimed that Gram had an affair with his father, and that he had loaned a great sum of money to her because he was in love with her and she was trying to get out from under Sophie and Mindy's grandfather's gambling debts. It was both hard to believe and nearly impossible to prove. Most of the people involved in the tale Mr. Summers was weaving were dead and gone. Still, none of that mattered for the present day. Mr. Summers was moving forward with a lawsuit. He wanted the store or the money owed, a sum that had yet to be determined—the way the interest was to be calculated was still subject to debate. One guess put it north of several hundred million dollars.

Mindy didn't have that kind of cash lying around. Sophie and Emma didn't, either. There was a big difference between a person's net worth and the size of a check they were able to write. Regardless of what happened, the Eden sisters had a huge legal battle on their hands and if things didn't go their way, a massive financial problem to fix. One that could destroy their grandmother's legacy. In that scenario, Mindy worried most about Sophie. Both her heart and her sense of self were wrapped so tightly around the store, it was impossible to know where one started and the other ended.

For now, Mindy couldn't entertain worries about Eden's. She was on her way to Sam's to help him with his speech for the fundraiser. There was a lot riding on Friday night, especially since Mindy had slipped up and not only told Sophie and Emma about the event, but then dared to tell them to attend it. All sorts of things could go wrong, like Jake and Sam getting into another staring contest, but Mindy had no choice. If the gap between her family and Sam wasn't bridged in some way, it would never, ever work. No, she didn't know if Sam was built for love or marriage, and she had the same reservations about herself, but she couldn't bear to think of the alternative—walking away from him. They'd made so much progress. She had to keep trying.

He buzzed her into the building as soon as she arrived and was waiting, wineglass in hand, when the elevator doors opened into his apartment. "I hope you're ready to work."

Mindy's first thought was that she wanted to get to work on Sam's shirt, but she had to focus. She stepped inside and let him take off her coat. "Of course. That's what I'm here for."

"Good. Because my writing is a disaster."

"I'm sure it's great. I'm sure you're overreacting."

"I'm not. I read it over the phone to Isabel. She told me it stinks."

Mindy placed her hands on both of Sam's biceps, telling herself this was not the time to give them a playful squeeze, however much she wanted to. "It's going to be okay. I'll stay all night if I have to."

He knocked back the last of his wine and grabbed the bottle from the kitchen counter, refilling his glass. "This is not my area of expertise. I'm not good at pulling heartstrings. And that's what this requires. If I'm going to get people to open their checkbooks, I need to leave an entire roomful of people in tears."

"Stop making excuses and show me what we're working with, okay?"

Sam waved Mindy into the living room and they headed up the stairs into the library, where his home office sat at one end of the loft. He pointed to his laptop, which was sitting on the desk. "Go ahead. Take a look. I'll be over here, dying a quiet death."

Mindy laughed quietly. She thought Sophie could be dramatic. Sam was giving her a solid run for her money. She pulled back his black leather desk chair and took a seat in front of his computer. She read carefully, trying to imagine Sam standing onstage behind a podium, looking as handsome as he had the day of Sophie's wedding, delivering these words he'd written. His work was indeed well composed, but this was not the sort of speech that would leave anyone clamoring for a tissue, and most certainly not their wallet. It was too clinical. Too safe. Sam was hiding again, this time behind words.

She turned in the chair when she finished reading. He was a good ten feet away, sipping on wine and pacing back and forth in front of the book-shelves. "I told you. It's terrible. Be honest. Be brutal. I need it."

Mindy had to figure out how to frame this. She didn't want him to be discouraged. It would make it far too easy for him to back out of delivering this speech and she sensed that he needed this, however much he was putting up a fight. If he hadn't wanted to do it, he never would have run it by his sister. He never would have asked for Mindy's input. When Sam was certain, he acted, without hesitation.

"I think you need to tell some stories, Sam. I think you need to tell people how it felt to be in that situation, with your mom sick and your sister away at school, and your dad struggling with it in his own way."

He kneaded at his forehead, the most stressed she'd ever seen him. "I don't know where to start. There are a million stories, and the ones that are the most memorable are also the most painful. I'm not really in the right mental space to sit in front of a computer and just bleed."

Mindy grabbed his laptop and wheeled the desk chair in front of the leather recliner he loved so much. "You sit and I'll ask you questions and when you answer, I'll type out what you say. We can use that as a starting point."

"I don't know, Min. I was sort of hoping we could just have a nice night together. Drink some wine. Drink some more wine." He bobbed his eyebrows up and down.

She was absolutely on board for that, but they had to stay on track. "There will be plenty of time for that. Let's finish this first. The fundraiser is only two days away and you need to practice before then. If we don't get this done, you won't be able to be as polished as you want to be."

Sam bunched up his lips, scrutinizing her with his dark eyes. She wasn't sure what he was looking for, but she met his gaze with her own, unflinching. She was going to be here for him, but she was also going to drag this out of him if necessary. Even if

it took all night. "Okay. Fine. Let's get this done."
Sam plopped down in the leather chair and crossed
his long legs at the ankle. "What do you want to
know?"

Mindy hadn't experienced a lot of personal trag-
edy, but she did know pain. She did know what it
was to be vulnerable and helpless. She'd felt both
many times over the years. "Tell me about the first
time you cried about your mom's illness. The first
time you were pushed to the brink and you felt like
you couldn't take it anymore."

"Wow. You do not mess around."

"I know it sounds horrible, but this is the relat-
able moment. This is where people will hear your
words and see some part of themselves."

Sam avoided making eye contact, picking at his
pants leg. "It was the day I looked up ALS in the
library at school." His voice failed to carry its usual
strong timbre, but when he looked up at Mindy, she
could see on his face that his heart was doing the
heavy lifting here. "Our parents had told us that our
mom would get better, and I wanted to believe that.
But I didn't need to read very far before it became
obvious that it would take her life."

Mindy typed every word as he said it, not com-
menting, only letting him run. She was usually very
good at soldiering through hard work, but this was
a battle. All she wanted to do was cast aside the
computer and wrap him up in her arms.

"I remember there was a small group of students at one of the big tables. Four or five kids. Freshmen like me. They were talking. The librarian kept shushing them and they would snicker and laugh, then go back to having their fun. That was the first time it really hit me. They had this life that I'd once thought I had. And for me, it was gone. It was hard to imagine myself ever laughing or goofing around like them because there was this dark cloud moving in overhead. My mom was going to die. That was a fact and there was no getting past it. That seemed like it would never be me again. I guess it was innocence lost. I just grabbed my backpack and hightailed it out of there. I didn't even go back to class. I went straight home so I could spend time with my mom."

Mindy finished typing a few seconds after he stopped talking. It was good to have her hands occupied. She otherwise only wanted to hug Sam and take care of him. Tell him how sorry she was, even when she knew he didn't want her pity. "That must have been such a hard day."

"One of many."

"I've never been to this event, but is that the sort of thing people talk about?"

He cleared his throat. "It is."

"Okay. Then let's keep going."

Mindy pressed on and Sam talked, continuing through several other retellings of the events of his past. She marveled at how far he had come with her in a short amount of time. A few weeks ago, and certainly the first time they'd been together, he never would have done this. Part of her wanted to believe that it was the timing that was off the first time for them. He wasn't ready and she wasn't sure she had been, either. Were things finally coming together for them? Would it all work out? Friday was a big test. Then, like everything else in her life, she'd reevaluate and figure out her next step.

A few hours later, Sam had a working draft of the speech. He read it back to her from his laptop, and she did her best to stay objective and not get swayed by the emotion of the story. Still, it was impossible to not feel the pressure in the center of her chest, right in the vicinity of her heart.

"Practice a few more times and you'll be all set," she said. "You're going to do an incredible job. I know you will." Now that the speech was wrapped up, Mindy wanted to get herself wrapped up in Sam, but there were other things that needed to be addressed. She needed to tell him about her sisters coming to the event, even when she knew that he had trusted her to not say a thing. As to how he would react, she did not know. But she was done with having barriers between them. It all had to go.

Mindy had succeeded at something no one else had—she'd gotten Sam to shed his hard exterior.

Not even Isabel, who was especially good at getting people to do things they did not want to do, had ever been able to convince him that baring his soul was a good idea. He'd always been so convinced that letting down his guard would somehow make his pain worse. It wasn't better now, but it was different. Oddly, he felt more comfortable with it. And that was all because of Mindy.

"I really don't quite know how to thank you for this. I'm starting to feel like you're my therapist."

"Before you get too appreciative, you should know that I had to tell Sophie and Emma about the fundraiser."

Sam's stomach sank. One minute they were on the same wavelength, and the next they were running off the rails. "Why did you do that? I specifically asked you not to."

Mindy wheeled herself closer to his chair and took his hands. "I know. And it was my intention to honor that. But I didn't want to hide the fact that you and I had spent the week together."

"Despite the bet?"

"Yes. Even with the bet. So I spilled that detail and, of course, they protested."

Sam couldn't listen to this. He got up out of his seat and distanced himself from her, but something stopped him when he got only a few feet. "Of course they did. They hate me, Min. I don't see how we're ever supposed to get past that."

Mindy rushed up to him and forced him to look her in the eye. "They don't hate you. They don't hate the real you because they don't know the real you. That's why I told them."

"I don't need their sympathy. I don't need anyone's."

"I know that. But I need them to see you the way I see you. Or at least some of the way I see you. Which is why I also asked them to come to the event."

Sam could hardly believe what she was saying. "You did what? Is Jake coming?"

Mindy shrugged sheepishly. "I guess? I don't know for sure."

Again, Sam needed his space, and he took it, doubling back to his chair, picking up his laptop and returning it to the desk. "I can't believe this. I shouldn't have agreed to any of this. It was a mistake."

"Sam. Don't shut me out. Listen to me. Please." Mindy didn't let him off the hook, storming up right behind him. She gripped his shoulders and leaned into his back, pulling him against her. "I know this is going to be hard, but I want you to do it for us."

Sam stood frozen, keenly aware of his breaths as they shuddered in and out of his lungs. *Us.* She said *us.* "For us?" He turned and circled his arms around her. "Is that what this is? Because it feels like I'm the one who's going to be on trial with everyone there."

"Hey. I'm on trial here, too. My sisters are convinced I've made a bad choice. And I need to prove them wrong. Because if you're going to be in my life, Sam, I need it to work with my family. There is no compromise that works for me. All or nothing."

Sam wasn't quite sure what emotion he was supposed to be feeling right now. There were bits of hope running around in his head—Mindy had suggested she wanted him in her life. But she'd also suggested it wouldn't work if her family didn't approve. And it was difficult to be content with that. There was part of him that wanted her to risk it all for him, even when he knew that was foolish. It seemed like that was the only way to know it was real. It seemed like the only sure sign of love.

"Do you want to know what happened between Jake and me?" he asked.

Mindy's eyes went wide with surprise. "If you want to tell me, of course I do."

"I did cut him out of the deal. He's not wrong about that. But I did it so I could pay back the insurance company the claim on my father's life insurance. I couldn't live with myself, knowing that I'd received any reward at all for his death. And I couldn't let Isabel live with it, either. My conscience needed a clean slate and I saw an opportunity and I took it. So when I told you that I did it to help some-one, I was helping me."

Mindy clasped her hand over her mouth. "Oh, my God, Sam. You did that?"

He nodded, willing the shame to go away. "If I would have known how much trouble it was going to cost down the road, I wouldn't have done it. I guess I figured that Jake would eventually forgive me. But he put up such a wall after that happened, there was no way for me to get back in."

"Jake has his own issues," Mindy said. "He grew up with a horrible home life and his mother aban-doned him with his grandmother, who was not a nice woman. I'm sure he simply can't handle be-trayal."

Sam clamped his eyes closed, letting his mis-takes tumble around in his head. "I had no idea. He never told me."

"That's the problem here. People don't tell each other stuff. And then it ends up getting one hun-dred times worse. Do you want me to tell Sophie and ask her to tell Jake?"

Sam shook his head. "No. If they're coming on Friday night, I'll do it myself. It has to be man-to-man. Either he'll forgive me or he won't. I can't focus on what other people think, even if it is your family, Mindy. Even if they might never let me have a moment's peace."

"Okay. Whatever you think is right."

"Just so you know, I'm not the only one who's going to fall under some scrutiny at the fundraiser. Isabel is going to be there and I'm afraid that her opinion of you isn't much better than what your sisters think of me."

Mindy sucked in a deep breath, her shoulders rising up near her ears. "Oh, God. She's going to put me on the spot, isn't she?"

"Probably. That's her personality. I mean, she's mostly harmless, but I'm not saying it won't hurt. It might. She doesn't have a great opinion of the Eden family in general, but most of that falls on you."

Mindy wrapped her arms around her midsection as if she was trying to shore up her defenses. "I'm getting a stomachache just thinking about it. Why did you have to tell me this? I might have been better off if it was a sneak attack."

Sam pulled her into a hug, rocking her back and forth. He didn't want to torment her, but he didn't mind giving her a small taste of what he lived with on an everyday basis. He'd shielded her from Isabel before. That couldn't happen anymore. Not if they had any shot at all of a future. "If I have to worry for two days about what will happen, then you do, too. Plus, now you know how it feels to go without the unwavering support of family."

"This feels a little bit like payback."

"I'd say it's more like the final test." He reached up and smoothed her hair, committing the feeling of the silky strands beneath his fingers to memory. If things didn't work out between them, he could look back on this moment and try to cling to it.

"Now who's the one with the bad bedside manner? That does not make me feel any better. At all."

He knew it was harsh, but he'd grown accustomed to dealing with some pretty damn unpleasant things lately. Now was no time to quit. "It's our shared reality, Mindy. Either our families decide to get in line on Friday night, or they continue to get in the way. And if that's the case, it'll be time for you and me both to decide if we were just having fun or if we're willing to go to battle with the people we love most." He hated putting that spin on it, but in many ways, he was only filling in the blanks for her. He might be willing to go against Isabel in the end, but he feared Mindy would never shake the iron grip of her family. They were both better off if it was out in the open.

"I know. You're right."

If only she knew he took zero solace in that fact. "Will you stay tonight? I don't want you to go."

"I don't have any clothes with me. No toothbrush."

"No excuses tonight, remember? That's what you told me about the speech." When it came to excuses, he had no more when it came to the real confession he wanted to make—that he loved her. The words were right on his lips, waiting to be uttered. But this wasn't the right time. They still had their hurdles ahead. If he went down in flames on Friday, she would likely side with her family. Which meant that all he could do was cherish tonight with Mindy. It was the only certain thing he had to hold on to.

Twelve

The fundraiser was being held at a midtown art museum. The event space was beautifully appointed—fifty round tables dotted the room, all topped with candles and ruby-red floral centerpieces, just waiting for the hundreds of guests to arrive at any minute. Sam's mood did not reflect the relative calm and elegance of the room he was standing in. In fact, he was already freaking out. He paced back and forth in front of one of the bar stations while a bartender dumped ice into bins and waiters polished glassware.

Ms. Parson, the charity's representative, the woman Sam had given such a hard time when she'd called him at the office, approached. "Are you sure you're okay, Mr. Blackwell?" She peered up at him from behind frameless glasses, seeming nothing short of gravely concerned.

"Yes. Absolutely. Just going over the speech in my head. No problems at all." He had to lie. He'd already put Ms. Parson through the wringer.

"Okay, then. I'm going to go back and check with the caterer on a few things. I believe they have just opened the doors. Guests will be arriving any second now."

Great. That's not helping. "Perfect. Thank you."

Isabel had apparently been one of the first people through the door. She marched up to him in a stylish white gown with silvery beads, her long black hair back in a sleek ponytail. "If it isn't the man of the hour," she said, kissing him on the cheek.

"Do not call me that. That's the exact last thing I want to be."

"All ready to give your speech?"

"As ready as I will ever be. Which isn't saying a lot, but it's better than nothing."

"When do you have to get up and speak?"

"It's the first thing, but they wait about an hour, until everyone has a few cocktails in them. After that, it's dinner and dancing."

"They probably worry people will eat and take off. Gotta put on the thumbscrews as early as possible."

The thought of medieval torture was a nice one

right now. He'd much rather have dealt with that than anything else. "I'm glad you could be here. I appreciate you coming." Sam had to decide how to best frame what he had to say to his sister. "Mindy's going to be here tonight and I'd like to introduce you two. I'm hoping you can find it in your heart to be nice."

"This is definitely a thing, isn't it? Not just a fling? Are you sure you want to go there? What if she spins you out of her life again?"

Sam could handle only so many questions at one time, especially questions for which he had few answers. "Yes, it's a thing. I like her a lot. In fact, I think I love her." Sam choked back the admission. He hadn't said it out loud before that moment.

Isabel grinned and elbowed him in the stomach. "You're such a sap. It's adorable."

"I thought you didn't like Mindy."

"Oh, I don't. I mean, I won't if she does one single thing to hurt you. But if you've fallen in love, of course I support that." She smoothed Sam's lapel and patted him on the shoulder. "Just be careful. These Eden women are not to be trifled with."

Sam knew that very well. And he was not certain about what she would say if he finally just made his admission. Would she think he was softhearted like his sister did? She was not a woman who got wrapped up in typical romantic gestures—she was the sort of woman who swooned when you sold her a building. And as her mother had pointed out, she was also someone who viewed commitment as a trap. Although Sam was buying that line of thinking less and less. He suspected that Mindy's mother didn't know her like he did. The woman who was willing to stay up all night to write a speech, or was willing to push him past his comfort zone, was not a person who shied away from the more complicated things in life. And if anything was complicated, it was love.

"Speak of the devil," Isabel muttered under her breath. "Your lovely date and her sister are fast approaching. Along with your nemesis, Jake Wheeler."

"He's not my nemesis. He's just stubborn. I don't need everyone in the whole world to be my friend." Except that he did need to patch things up with Jake. He was part and parcel of the Eden clan.

Sam chose to focus on Mindy as she approached, and what a sight she was in a stunning black gown that shimmered in the candlelight. She'd worn her hair up in a twist similar to the one she wore to Sophie's wedding. He only hoped he'd have the chance to later take it out exactly like he had the first time.

Mindy winked at him when she was about ten feet away, then went right in for a kiss. Sam was stuck between getting what he wanted, that close physical contact with Mindy, and the audience who was witnessing it. This was more than just a kiss. She was showing her sister and his that she meant business about him. He had to wonder if she had any idea how comforting that was to him. It was like taking fifty deep breaths.

"Hi," she muttered against his lips. "You look very handsome tonight."

"You look incredible. Absolutely gorgeous. I want you to meet my sister, Isabel."

Isabel did her sisterly duty, but Sam could tell that her smile was an act. Behind it was Isabel the protector, the one who would not let him get hurt. He wanted to tell her to back off, but he knew it was of little use. "It's nice to meet you, Mindy, after talking to you on the phone while you were staying with Sam."

Isabel glanced over at Sophie and Jake and went right ahead and introduced herself. "Hi, I'm Isabel Blackwell. Sam's sister."

"Sophie Eden. This is my husband, Jake Wheeler," Sophie said, seeming confused by everything going on before them. "I'm Mindy's sister."

"Oh, I know," Isabel said.

Sam both hated and loved his sister for pushing the envelope. Isabel knew very well the undercurrents between this group of people. She knew that Sophie's and Jake's opinion of him had caused Mindy to break up with him before. She wasn't testing the boundaries for spite. She was testing them to make sure they didn't break.

Sam wasn't particularly keen on talking to Jake

after the run-in the night of the rehearsal dinner, but he also didn't want to let their feud go on any longer. "Jake. Hey. Nice to see you. Thank you for coming tonight."

Jake did offer a handshake with a minimum of hesitation. That was a positive sign. "Sam. I had no idea you were so involved with charity."

Sam nodded. "Well, I am. And I'm making more of a point of putting these things out in the open."

Isabel took Sam's arm and snugged herself close for an instant. "I'd say it's more a matter of him not wanting to brag about himself. He's been doing it for years."

"I wish I'd seen this side of you before," Sophie said, still seeming entirely skeptical.

"All I can tell you, Sophie, is that I will try to do better." He put his arm around Mindy, hoping Sophie would catch the double meaning. He was trying to do better on all fronts. "Speaking of which, Jake, I was hoping that you and I could get together some time soon. Maybe grab a drink. Hash out a few things."

Jake looked to Sophie, almost as if he was seeking her approval. Mindy might have been the oldest of the sisters, but Sophie played the role of matriarch. "That could be good," Sophie said, again sounding uncertain. "As long as it fits in your schedule, of course."

Jake turned back to Sam. "I'll have to take a look at my calendar."

Sam wasn't about to make any more of an overture than that. He'd tried to extend the olive branch. It was up to Jake to take it.

"How soon until you have to make your speech?" Mindy asked.

Sam glanced at his Rolex. "Half hour or so."

"Do you have a minute to talk?" she asked. "Just the two of us?"

Sam couldn't think of anything he wanted more than to be alone with Mindy. "Yes. Of course." He took her hand and led her to the far corner of the room, away from the bustle and noise of the crowd.

"I debated about whether or not I should kiss you in front of my sister and Jake. But you know what? The second I saw you, I knew that it was stupid to not kiss you. I want to kiss you. I should just kiss you, right?"

Sam had to laugh. "Yes. You should kiss me whenever you want. I'm hoping it's often."

She gathered both of his hands in hers and squeezed them tight. "You are going to rock this speech. I know you will. And then we can drink a bunch of wine when you're done and say mean-spirited things about our siblings behind their backs."

He pulled her against him in a snug embrace. "You are so funny." *I love you.* It was right there.

Within reach. "I think you did pretty well with Isabel."

"Something tells me she won't be quite so nice if you're not around."

"I will do my best to keep you safe." He muttered the words against her ear, meaning it in a much greater sense than the here and now. He wanted the chance to do it for the long haul.

"I'm glad you made an effort with Jake. I think he'll come around eventually. I really do."

"What about Sophie? Do you think she's given up on the bet? I should hope so."

Mindy shook her head slightly. "Giving up on the bet would mean giving up on me staying at Eden's, and that's the last thing she's going to do. But that's okay. You know, I'm over it. My sister and I will reach an understanding somehow. Some way. We always do. There might be some yelling and hair pulling, but that's nothing new."

"Hmm. Now this hair pulling, is that something I can watch?"

Mindy smacked his arm. "Be serious. You have to put on a straight face in a few minutes."

"Don't remind me."

"Oh, come on. You'll be perfect. I know it." She leaned into him and gave him a big kiss. "Daniel and Emma just got here, so I should go say hi. And we need to find our table. I'll talk to you after you're done?"

"You will be my reward." *In more ways than one.*

Sam watched as Mindy sauntered off. She was a truly remarkable woman. Strong and smart, funny and sexy. He'd be a fool if he didn't put everything on the line for her. The how and when were still up in the air, but he knew it had to be soon. She wouldn't wait on him forever.

Sam crossed over to the other side of the room and checked in with Ms. Parson.

"I'd say it's time for you to go on up and welcome everyone and make our first big pitch of the night for donations."

"Got it. Thank you for the opportunity," he said, shaking her hand.

She knocked her head to one side quizzically. "It's you I should be thanking, Mr. Blackwell."

He shook his head. "No. I'm sure I got it right the first time. And please, call me Sam."

Her face lit up with a ready smile. "Break a leg, Sam."

Sam took the stairs up onto the stage, squinting into the bright lights. He took deep breaths as the music faded, reminding himself that no matter what, he would get through it. He had been through things more difficult. This would be over in a matter of minutes and he would ultimately wonder why he'd ever allowed himself to get so worked up about it. As he looked out into the crowd, full of expectant faces about to hang on his every word, his heart thundered in his chest. He had to orient himself, search for the table where Mindy sat with her family. Two rows back. On the right-hand side of the room. He found it and his sights flew right to her. There she was in that heartbreaking dress, looking more beautiful than ever. How was that possible? For a woman to be more gorgeous now than even a week ago? A minute ago? Was it because he knew what was behind the beautiful shell? Was it because he truly knew now what she was made of?

The answer to those questions was an absolute and resounding "yes." And so he did what he had to do. He adjusted the microphone, took a sip of water and prepared himself to throw away the speech he'd written with Mindy. Tonight he had a different plan.

Mindy shifted in her seat as Sam stood on the stage, the audience eerily quiet. Mindy's pulse pounded, making it hard to hear. She wished she could send Sam a psychic message. *You'll do great. I believe in you.*

It was almost as if he'd heard her thoughts. His gaze connected with hers and he seemed to say something in return. Something along the lines of how they had done this together. How this might be his night, but she'd helped him get here. She couldn't have been more proud.

"Good evening, I'm Sam Blackwell. I'm honored to be here tonight to share the story of my family's struggle with ALS. I'm not the sort of guy who opens up, so I hope you all take notice, especially when I ask you to be as generous as humanly possible this evening. Because I am going to ask that of you. Each and every one of you." Sam methodically pointed to a few people around the room, and everyone started to laugh, lightening the mood. "And with that, I'll get started."

The speech Sam and Mindy had written together rolled smoothly from his mouth. He was as confident as could be, and Mindy could not have been any more proud. He delivered the heartbreaking stories about how he had to watch his mother's decline and the way his father had struggled with watching his wife fade before his very eyes. He spoke of Isabel. He spoke of being on his own. He spoke of love.

"And years later, after having gone through that unbelievable loss, I had to ask myself where the love in my life was. Had it disappeared?"

Mindy sat, transfixed. This was not part of the speech they had written. Sam had gone off script. And she had to wonder where in the world he was going with all of this.

"Yes, I had my sister, but she has her own life. And the love I have inside me is bigger than one person. I no longer had my parents. And although I love them every day from afar, there's still a surplus. There's something in my heart that's about to burst. Every day. I think we all experience that on some level, and it's impossible to measure the emptiness it creates when you have love in your heart and there's nowhere for it to go."

Sam took a sip of his water and let out a breathy laugh. He lowered his mouth to the microphone and said, "I'm sure you're all wondering where I'm going with this."

The crowd laughed in kind, as did Mindy, nervously. Where was he going?

"I've learned a lot about myself while preparing for tonight. I'd once thought of the journey I made with my family as a dead end. But the truth is that experiencing it for a second time while writing this speech, I realized that it was only a single point in my life. That there was more ahead if I just opened my heart to it. I needed a very special woman to show me how to do that, and I couldn't be more thankful to her if I tried. She not only makes me a better person, she makes me the sort of person who gets up in front of a room of strangers and asks them to write a big fat check."

Again, the audience laughed. Meanwhile, Sophie caught Mindy's attention by bugging her eyes. Mindy shrugged. What was she supposed to say? Sam had gone so far out on a limb. In front of her entire family. In front of these people he'd once been afraid to open up to. And he was putting it all on the line in the most public way possible, probably because that was what their relationship had become—too many people weighing in, too many people deciding they had a voice. It was best to put it all out there. For the people who knew them and cared about them, they would know what he was talking about. They knew the context and what this meant.

"So in closing, just remember what brought us all here tonight. It isn't a disease that brought us together. It's not sad stories, and it's not the promise of finding a cure. It's love. Love made us walk through the door tonight and open ourselves up to the possibilities. Take your loved ones and hold them close. Make sure that they know what they mean to you. And let everything in your heart free. Thank you."

Sam had hardly finished uttering that final syllable when the audience rose to their feet en masse and erupted in thunderous applause. Sam looked out over the crowd in Mindy's direction, and their gazes connected. It was a miraculous moment and not just because Mindy could hardly see, the tears absolutely pouring from her eyes. How he managed to smile at her after the speech he'd just delivered, she did not know. But that was Sam—always surprising her with his amazing ways. He walked down off the stage, only to be greeted by a throng of people who had left their tables to shake his hand.

Mindy had to get to him right away. She had to tell him that she loved him. She couldn't let him go another minute wondering if she did.

"Mindy. Wait." Sophie grabbed her arm. "Is he talking about you?"

"If he isn't, I'm about to put my foot in my mouth, big-time."

"You guys are in love? You didn't tell me that the other day when we talked about it."

"I know. I guess I was just too scared to admit it."

"Oh, Mindy. You had to know that I would let you out of the bet if you really wanted that. I'm not going to hold you hostage."

Mindy leaned over and kissed her sister on the cheek. "Thank you. I appreciate that. But that's not what I mean. I was scared to tell you I love him because I couldn't tell you that he would ever say it back. I was a big chicken."

"And now?"

"And now it's time for me to put it all on the line." Mindy wound her way past the tables, dodging waiters and other guests, until she was standing outside a ring of people waiting to talk to Sam.

He saw her and smiled, then reached past several guests for her. She put her hand in his, which left her with a tingle. That zap of electricity. It would never grow old. He pulled her through until she was right by his side. "I'm sorry. I know we need to talk. This will only take a second. I promise."

"It's fine. I'm not going anywhere." She held on to his hand like it was her lifeline, and in many ways it was. No, she hadn't fully talked this through with

Sophie, but quite frankly, she didn't plan to. Sam was the right man for her. She knew that with every bone in her body.

As the crowd around Sam dwindled, Mindy spotted her sister and Jake standing on the periphery. She certainly hoped there would be nothing but well-wishes from them. Sam deserved nothing less.

Jake pushed forward and held out his hand to shake Sam's. "Incredible speech. Absolutely amazing."

"Thank you. I appreciate that."

"I, uh… I'm sorry about earlier. I'm sorry about the wedding. I would like to have coffee. I would like to see if we can patch things up."

Sam smiled wide. "Sounds like a plan. I will give you a call in a day or two."

Jake cast his sights at Mindy. "No hurry. I have a feeling you have other things you need to deal with."

Sam squeezed Mindy's hand. "I do. In fact, right now." He leaned down and muttered in her ear, his breath warm against her neck. "We have to go somewhere where we can talk."

"God, yes." Mindy led the charge, towing Sam back to the entrance and right outside into the night air.

"I will have to go back in at some point," he said.

"I love you, Sam." She didn't want to wait any longer. She didn't want any more buildup to the words that should have come out of her mouth before. "I loved you before you made that speech. And I don't know why I was scared to say it other than I feared that you might not return the words and that was going to crush my heart."

"Shh. Shh. It's okay." Sam placed a hand on each side of her head and kissed her on the lips, making Mindy rise up onto her tiptoes just to be closer. "I love you, sweet woman. I love you more than I ever thought possible. And I'm just as guilty of holding back. At first it was your family, then the bet, but in the end, I think it was all that same fear. I worried that I wouldn't be enough. I worried that I wouldn't be right for you."

Mindy smiled so wide her lips hurt, her chest heaving with happiness. "I'm so glad you said all of those things in front of everyone. It was perfect. We had to put everyone on notice, and you did that. Now we let the chips fall where they may. I defy anyone to tell us that we don't deserve to be in love."

Sam arched both eyebrows at her. "I am very happy to hear you say that. I was worried you would get angry with me and say that I put you on the spot with your sisters, but I also figured that there was no way things were going to get any worse, right?"

"Absolutely right."

Sam sighed and wrapped his arms around her. "You know what?"

"What?"

"I'm happy. Actually, completely and totally happy. I can't think of a single thing in the entire world that I would want right now."

"Nothing?" Mindy asked with a pointed stare.

Sam laughed. "Well, yeah, of course. That." He tugged her even closer and kissed her softly. "I always want that from you."

"I suppose we have to go back inside first, though, huh? Say our goodbyes. Let people fawn all over you."

He took her hand, leading her back to the museum steps. "I say one more hour. Then I want you to come home with me, Mindy."

Her heart absolutely swelled, right there in the center of her chest. "I'll come home if you promise me one thing," she said, stopping right in front of the door.

"What's that?"

"That you'll clean out one side of your closet. If I'm coming home with you, I'm staying. For good."

Epilogue

One month after the fundraiser, so much in life had changed. For starters, the renovations on the BMO offices had begun. As had the restructuring of the company, starting with Mindy installing Carla Meadows as the new CEO after Carla cleverly not only got Matthew to admit he was trying to undermine the value of the company, but also ask if he could bribe her to help him. The best part? Carla had been smart enough to record the whole conversation on her phone. Pushing Matthew out of the picture had ultimately proved a very simple thing, just as Sam had suggested.

Sam and Mindy were at the Mercer late Saturday

morning to check out the progress. The first floor had been completely cleaned out and had all-new industrial lighting and a fresh coat of paint. Soon enough they would start moving the printers in, as well as the shipping department. The second, third and fourth floors were also well under way with refinished floors and a more open layout after knocking down many walls. But Mindy was most excited to see the top floor. Where her office would be. They reached number five and, although it was still weeks away from being complete, Mindy could see the space taking shape. They'd installed glass walls for her office, right in the sunniest corner. It would be a very cheery place to work.

Sam put his arm around her while they surveyed her little kingdom together. "You must be proud," he said.

"Still a long way to go, but yes. I'm feeling a big sense of accomplishment right now."

To Mindy, this felt like a very full-circle moment. This old building that had once seemed like nothing more than a pawn in a complicated game of business had really brought her and Sam back together again. She might hate Matthew Hawkins for what he tried to do, but she had to appreciate him on some level. If he hadn't tried his underhanded trick, there was no telling if Mindy would have ever been smart enough to try again with Sam. She worried that she wouldn't have dared to cross her sisters. Now she was so glad she had.

"And maybe a little bit of relief?" he asked.

"More like a whole lot. The Matthew thing is resolved. Sophie backed off the bet. Technically, I'm free to do whatever I want in a year."

"But?" he asked. "I'm sensing a *but* at the end of that sentence."

"But I feel guilty. And I feel bad. Will I just be abandoning Sophie and Emma? What about this Benjamin Summers guy and the lawsuit? What if we end up losing the store?" Mindy knew she sounded frantic, but that was the one unsettled area of her life. Yes, it was a big improvement over a month or two ago when her entire existence was in disarray. But still, she didn't like having such a big thread dangling.

"First off, I don't want you to feel guilty. If you make it to the end of the two years, you can still decide to stay at the store. A lot could happen in twelve months. There's no telling where you'll be."

"You're right. Things change. They always do." Mindy gnawed on her fingernail. "I think I'm going to need some lawyer recommendations from you for Eden's. Our in-house legal team plays it totally by the book and I think we're going to need to out-maneuver the issue of this lien against the store."

"So you come to me for the less-by-the-book people?"

"You know what I mean."

He chuckled warmly. God, she loved that sound. Happy Sam Blackwell was the absolute best. "I actually have an idea, but I think it'll be more than a little controversial."

"Oh, good. Just what you and I need. Controversy."

He dropped his arm from her shoulder and stood to face her. "Just promise me you'll hear me out."

"I promise."

"Isabel."

Mindy blinked. "As in your sister?"

"She's an unbelievable lawyer and she's made the decision to move to New York. She could handle this thing no problem. I swear."

Mindy had not been prepared for this idea at all. "I don't know. My family has just gotten used to one Blackwell. I'm not sure the idea of putting the fate of the store in the hands of your sister is going to fly."

Sam shrugged. "Think about it. I know she could do an amazing job."

Mindy would have to ponder that thoroughly, as well as find a way to run it by Sophie and Emma. "Okay. I will."

"Ready to head out?" Sam asked. "I was thinking we should go for a drive. It's such a beautiful day."

With nothing else planned aside from a quiet dinner at home, Mindy was game. "Sure. Sounds fun."

They locked up the building when they got downstairs and walked over to where Sam had parked his Bugatti, near the loading dock. He'd said that he wanted to give his driver the day off, but Mindy also wondered if he'd just used this excursion as an excuse to drive. He loved his car, and living in the city didn't make it a very practical choice.

He drove north and eventually hopped on the Palisades Interstate Parkway, which ran parallel to the Hudson River. She just enjoyed the colorful scenery of a late-autumn day, but after about a half hour, Mindy had to ask, "Where are we going? I can't help but feel like you have a destination in mind."

"I have something I want to show you." He glanced over at her, but his eyes were hidden behind sunglasses, revealing nothing.

"Something like what?"

"It's a surprise. We'll be there in a few minutes, okay? Just relax. I promise you it's a good thing."

Mindy sat back in the seat. She wasn't big on surprises, but she figured that whatever Sam had up his sleeve had to be something she would like. He'd figured her out pretty well by now. After another ten or fifteen minutes, he pulled off the main road and they were soon in a residential area with sprawling lawns and extravagant, elegant homes. He turned on a side street and pulled up in front of a house at the very end of the road. He put the car in Park and killed the engine, then turned to her.

"Well? What do you think?"

Mindy looked out the window. "It's beautiful. And massive. And way outside the city." She turned back to him. "Do you know the person who lives here?"

He shook his head and removed his sunglasses. "No. But I know the person who wants to live here. And I know the person he's hoping will move in with him."

Mindy didn't want to be slow to figure this out, but this wasn't adding up. "What are you saying, Sam?"

"Come on. Let's get out of the car and take a look."

"Okay." Mindy climbed out and joined Sam as they walked up to the gate. The house was still very far away, down at the end of a long cobblestone drive. There was a stone fountain in the center of a large courtyard, manicured landscaping as far as the eye could see. Dozens of windows dotted the front of the home, suggesting that there were an awful lot of rooms.

"I'm sorry. I wish I had the keys so we could look at it," Sam said, gripping the wrought-iron gate. "Although part of me doesn't want to look at it if you aren't into the idea."

"You're saying you want to buy this house?"

"I'm saying that I want to know what's next for us. I guess I'm asking you what's next. I found out the other day that this house was for sale and I looked at it on the website and all I could think is that I loved the idea of getting out of the city, and I loved the idea of doing that with you."

"Oh, my gosh. That's amazing. And also a little surprising. What exactly would we put in a house that big, Sam?"

He shrugged. "I don't know. Kids? A bunch of pets? We could do whatever we want."

Kids. Wow. That was a leap she had not seen coming. Forget work priorities, she would need to rethink everything. Still, she turned to Sam and her heart melted. It was a lovely idea, especially with him. She suspected he was eager to build the family he'd always wanted, so he could remember the one he'd once had.

"You and I have spent so much time worrying about business and family," he said. "Now that we're together, I want to know where you see us going. I cleaned out half of my closet for you, but this would be a lot more than that."

Mindy cast her sights at him again. She would have been surprised, but she knew that they would eventually have the commitment talk. When she asked herself the question—what do you want?— the answer was him. She wanted him by her side every day. She wanted to be able to come home to him at night and wake up next to him the next morning. She wanted weekends and holidays, good times and bad. She wanted everything she could get from Sam. Every last drop. "You sound like you're unsure of what I want."

"It's always easiest if you tell me. I'm a man, Mindy. Not a mind reader."

"You're also a guy who overflows with confidence. You don't always have to follow my lead. Why don't you tell me what you want. You're entitled, you know."

Sam pressed his lips together and looked through the gate again, the breeze blowing his hair back from his face. He was so handsome in profile, his strong nose and jaw. The lips she loved to kiss. He turned back to her and she could see just how much he had dropped his defenses. A single tear rolled down his cheek. "I want the fairy-tale ending, Min. I want us to promise each other that we'll always be there for each other. And I want us to do it in front of everyone we love with rings and champagne and vows. I know you see marriage as a trap, but I promise you that I will never let it be that way for us. I will always be true. I will always be open and honest. I will always make sure you know that you're loved for the incredible woman you are."

Mindy stood perfectly still. This scene between her and Sam was so unimaginable the first time they were together, and the second, and the third… And that was all on her. She'd told herself she wanted him to stick around, but the truth was that it was only at the moments when he said he would that she ended up getting nervous.

But not anymore. That was the old Mindy. She was not letting Sam walk out on an emotional ledge without being there to catch him. "So you want to get married? Buy a big house and start having kids?"

He nodded. "I know it sounds ridiculous coming from me. I know this is probably the last thing you ever expected, but it is what I want. I love you, Mindy. From the moment I met you, there was no one else. We are meant for each other. We fit together perfectly."

Mindy leaned into him and gave him a kiss. "In more ways than one."

"So what do you say? With every other bit of uncertainty ahead, what do you say we place all bets on us?"

Mindy's heart felt as though it was doing cartwheels and backflips, a feeling she'd never expected to feel at the prospect of marriage. But she knew now that it wasn't about the institution or the promise, it was all about the man she loved more than anything. "I'll take that bet, Sam Blackwell. I'll take it every single day."

* * * * *